DANIEL
HALF
HUMAN

By DAVID CHOTJEWITZ
Translated by DORIS ORGEL

SIMON PULSE

NEW YORK   LONDON   TORONTO   SYDNEY

SIMON PULSE
An imprint of Simon & Schuster Children's Publishing Division
1230 Avenue of the Americas, New York, NY 10020
Text copyright (c) 2000 by CARLSEN Verlag GmbH, Hamburg
Translation copyright (c) 2004 by Simon & Schuster, Inc.
First published in Germany under the title *Daniel Halber Mensch*
Published by arrangement with CARLSEN Verlag GmbH, Hamburg
All rights reserved, including the right of reproduction in whole or in part in any form.
SIMON PULSE and colophon are registered trademarks of Simon & Schuster, Inc.
Also available in a Simon & Schuster Books for Young Readers hardcover edition titled *Daniel Half Human: And the Good Nazi*
Designed by Michael Nagin
The text of this book was set in Trade Gothic and Times New Roman.
Manufactured in the United States of America
First Simon Pulse edition March 2006
6 8 10 9 7
The Library of Congress has cataloged the hardcover edition as follows:
Chotjewitz, David.
[Daniel halber mensch. English]
Daniel, half human: and the good Nazi/David Chotjewitz ; translated by Doris Orgel.—1st ed. P. cm.
"A Richard Jackson Book."
Summary: In 1933, best friends Daniel and Armin admire Hitler, but as anti-Semitism buoys Hitler to power, Daniel learns he is half Jewish, threatening the friendship even as life in their beloved Hamburg, Germany, is becoming nightmarish. Also details Daniel and Armin's reunion in 1945 in interspersed chapters.
ISBN-13: 978-0-689-85747-8 (hc.)
ISBN-10: 0-689-85747-0 (hc.)
ISBN: 3-551-58045-6 (German ed., published by Carlsen Verlag in March 2000)
1. Germany—History—1933–1945—Juvenile fiction. [1. Germany—History—1933–1945—Fiction. 2. Nazis—Fiction. 3. Best friends—Fiction. 4. Friendship—Fiction. 5. Prejudices—Fiction. 6. Jews—Germany—History—1933–1945—Fiction.] I. Orgel, Doris. II. Title. PZ7.C446355Dan 2004
[Fic]—dc22
2003025554
ISBN-13: 978-0-689-85748-5 (pbk.)
ISBN-10: 0-689-85748-9 (pbk.)

ACKNOWLEDGMENTS

The work on this novel was supported by a grant from the Prussian Seehandlung Foundation.

THERE WAS NO MORE STREET, JUST A PATH through massive piles of rubble. My jeep couldn't get through. I put it in reverse, backtracked, and turned off to the right.

But where I'd expected to find the Grosse Bergstrasse, there was just another rubble field. To the left, down near the Elbe, there were blocks of walled-up, bombed-out houses. I stopped and got out. The jeep wouldn't block traffic, because there wasn't any.

I knew this city inside out, every inch of it by heart, but there was no more city—only ruins and a sea of bricks in all directions. Of the trees that had stood here, only blackened trunks remained. Some sprouted a few thin green twigs.

But there was life amidst the rubble. A woman wearing a man's torn jacket, a spotted apron over her belly, stood hanging up wash. She turned around, looked me over. Her face was pale. I wondered, *Do I know her?* She picked up the laundry basket and went into her shack.

The air was mild, soft against my skin.

Climbing back into the jeep, I asked myself, not for the first time, why had I landed here, in Hamburg, of all places? Shortly after Germany capitulated, I'd been transferred from my U.S. Army unit to the Royal British Army. They needed interpreters for special interrogations. But why didn't I ask to be stationed someplace else, say, on the Lüneburg Heath or in the Ruhr, anywhere at all, just, please, not Hamburg? And why, of all places, was I now heading toward the district of Altona? I had no job-related business there.

If this was once the Königstrasse, then in a few hundred meters I could turn left onto the Hoheschulstrasse . . . where the Christianeum was . . . where Dr. Knoppe used to torment us with Latin verbs, and make us translate endless passages from Julius Caesar's *Gallic Wars*. . . .

I suddenly remembered a delicious taste, a special fragrance. . . . My mouth began to water. And I almost heard the noise of cars rushing by on what had been a well-paved street. . . . These sharp memories took me back twelve years, to recess . . . sneaking out of the

2

schoolyard, me and Armin Hillmann . . . dashing across the intersection to the bakery on the Mühlenstrasse for our favorite midmorning snack— sweet, crumbly *Franzbrötchen*, a Hamburg specialty.

Now there was no more Hoheschulstrasse, no more Mühlenstrasse, and nothing left of that bakery, either. Just another path through rubble.

I followed it past makeshift barracks with tin roofs, past here and there a wooden cross and wilted flowers marking a grave. Now the air was thick and heavy. After I'd walked a few meters, my tongue felt coated with dust.

What was I looking for? I knew I wouldn't find the house. I could have driven on, to the Flottbeker Chaussee. That's where my family had lived.

It wasn't a clear thought, but deep inside myself I knew that whatever I was looking for, I didn't really want to find.

Among the few houses left halfway standing was one I recognized. In its basement was a bar called the Family Corner. Armin's father had sat here sometimes—once a week to be exact, on Tuesdays, when the dive where he hung out the rest of the time was closed.

No more door with glass panels. All there was were

3

wooden planks nailed shut. I stepped around some rubble to a side door and walked in.

Obviously, the Family Corner had not done any business for some time. But thanks to residues of beer, schnapps, sweat, and cigarettes lodged in the furniture and woodwork, the place still smelled like a dive.

Out of the corner of my eye I saw a slightly yellowed sign on the wall beside the coatrack: JEWS NOT INVITED.

In front of the bar crouched a heavyset man around fifty, hammering a bedframe together.

I didn't know him. Maybe the place had changed owners.

"Closed," he said in English. "No beer."

"Do you know what happened to the tenants in number seventeen?" I asked.

The man looked at me. People weren't used to a British officer speaking German.

"Number seventeen?"

"Yes, diagonally across from here."

He went to the window and stared out at the wreckage. Then he shrugged. "No idea. Everyone went into the air-raid shelter when the bombs were coming down."

"And then?"

"Moved away. Never came back. For what?" He looked at me more closely. "Don't I know you?" he asked. "Did you live on this street?"

"A little farther to the west," I answered. "But I spent a lot of time in this neighborhood."

He clearly wanted to get back to his work.

I asked, "Is there any way I can get through here to the Elbe?"

He looked past me toward the street.

"With that jeep? You'd have to drive all the way around the town hall. Here in Altona . . ." He shook his head and pounded another nail into the bedframe.

"Thanks," I said. I was already at the door when I noticed the sign again and turned back to him. "You forgot to take down the sign."

He rose to his feet with a groan. "What sign?"

I pointed.

He didn't know what to say. Since I made no move to leave, he went behind the bar, got a screwdriver, went over to the sign, and started to unscrew it.

I waved good-bye and left.

I crossed the street to number seventeen, where Armin had lived. I'd been here countless times. It was like a second home to me.

We two were an odd pair of friends. I lived on the Flottbeker Chaussee, a pinnacle of elegance toward which long stretches of lesser town houses aspired. My father was a highly regarded lawyer. We had two house-maids, a cook, and a nursemaid when I was little. The nursemaid played with me in our garden and would have stayed on even after I started school if I hadn't resisted strongly.

Whereas Armin lived here. A ruin now. I remem-bered the street the way it had been, narrow and wind-ing, with fish smells wafting from the harbor. Dockworkers, fish-factory workers, and people out of work who couldn't afford to feed their families lived here. Barely. At night whores too old to drum up busi-ness on the Reeperbahn stood around in courtyard entrances and alleys.

Armin's father was out of work. He sat in his reg-ular dive for hours on end with his beer glass in front of him, not drinking up so he wouldn't have to order another.

Like most people in this dirt-poor quarter, he was a "Red," an old Social Democrat, and none too pleased when his son made friends with a "rich brat" from the Flottbeker Chaussee. He liked it even less that we were passionately for "the movement." That's what the

6

Nazis were called back then, before they came to power.

I walked back to the jeep. The ground was strewn with bits of broken glass, chunks of cement, pieces of rusty metal. A green shard caught the sunlight. . . . I didn't let myself think back seven years to that November night when whole streets were littered with glass. No, I wasn't ready to relive Kristallnacht, the Night of Broken Glass. I thought back to only one glass splinter. Armin found it on the floor of the holding cell in the Victoriastrasse police station. "Look at that," he'd whispered.

And I remembered what my wrist looked like when we were in that holding cell: scratched and swollen, bright blood pushing through, forming little drops that stuck to the skin.

"There," Armin had said. "It worked."

PAINTING

THE AIR SMELLED OF COAL. A BITING WIND rose from the river, drove the thin snow over the pavement, and swept the smoke from the chimneys down into the courtyard.

Daniel kept looking left and right. It was so cold, his eyes were watering. The teardrops froze hard on his cheeks. He wiped his face with his glove, and then he heard something—faint, still far away. It sounded like marching. He knew right then that they were headed for trouble. Everything that could go wrong would. But all he said, not very loud, was, "This is crazy."

Armin's cap was pulled low over his face, his leather satchel tucked under one arm. In the dim light of the streetlamp he really did look like a dockworker heading home from the late shift. No one would have guessed that there were paintbrushes in the satchel. He was Daniel's age, just thirteen, but tall and sturdy. On him, the disguise looked convincing. On Daniel, not, because he was smaller, skinnier, could still pass for eleven and travel half-fare on the U-Bahn.

The rumpled jacket and workman's cap somehow looked all wrong on him. Besides, Armin had stuck him with the thankless job of carrying the paint bucket again.

Armin was already at the next street corner. He pushed his cap up a bit, took a casual look around, came sauntering back, and turned into the courtyard. The front building had people living in it; the buildings in the back were dilapidated, empty.

"This is crazy," Daniel said, louder. "And I'm freezing."

Armin snorted, went over to the crumbling side-wall.

Twelve brave Nazi fighters had lain dead in a street near here one Sunday in July last year. Daniel thought of them now. Again he looked carefully in all directions. Then, struggling with the heavy paint bucket, he sighed and followed Armin.

It really was insanity to go painting on walls here. But their honor was at stake, it *had* to be done, after what had happened earlier.

That morning some boys from the Communist Youth had come to the Christianeum. They'd stood at the entrance and passed out cheap-looking leaflets with dastardly slurs against Hitler's private army, the SA. Such provocation could not go unanswered.

The Christianeum, after all, was an elite

Gymnasium, attended by the sons of industrialists and state officials. Almost everyone in Daniel's class wanted to join the Hitler Jugend. And almost everyone thought that retaliatory action should be taken. Only what?

Peter Mehlhorn, class spokesman, had proposed: "Let's march over to the public high school this afternoon. We'll give those hoodlums a thrashing."

"Good idea," Armin said. "Except they don't have school on Saturdays."

Then a discussion started that would have gone on forever if the bell hadn't rung and recess hadn't ended. There were too many opinions, too many sissies, Armin told Daniel on the way to class. Too many mama's boys, scared of the least little brawl. And one Jew, Julius Cohn, whose father was a watchmaker in the Grosse Bergstrasse. "Nothing wrong with Julius, except he's for the German Nationalists, and they're a bunch of bourgeois decadents who don't like Hitler," Armin scoffed. "Typical," he said to Daniel. "Lots of talk and nothing comes of it."

He'd made up his mind: "It's up to us to do something. We'll be famous, you and me."

Daniel didn't like the idea. But he couldn't think of a way to argue against it without seeming a "bourgeois decadent" himself.

"We'll paint," Armin said.

Daniel took a deep breath. Going out into the

night disguised as grown-ups, painting swastikas on walls, was a big test of courage.

They'd done it before, he and Armin, dressed as a couple on a date (Armin's idea, and naturally, Daniel had had to be the girl). They'd gotten away with it. A *Schupo* out patrolling had passed right by and not suspected anything.

"This time we'll paint in the Johannisstrasse," Armin said.

The Johannisstrasse was in the working-class district, ruled by Reds. The Nazis called it "Little Moscow." To paint on walls there was asking for trouble, Daniel knew. But holding on to Armin's friendship was worth any risk.

That was why he'd asked and asked, pestering his mother till she finally gave in. "All right, you can sleep over at Armin's."

Just before midnight they'd put on some old clothes of Armin's father's and slipped out.

Of course, there were always police patrols. But Armin knew secret byways, dim-lit, steeply rising streets on which you were unlikely to run into any *Schupos*.

Entering the passageway that led into the courtyard, Daniel saw that the walls were covered with posters, mostly of hammers and sickles, and some with the Social Democrats' white arrows on red backgrounds, and their slogan: A VOTE FOR HITLER IS A VOTE FOR WAR.

Again he heard the sound of marching and felt chilled to the bone. Suddenly Armin's casual manner seemed absurd. It made him angry.

Nevertheless, he followed and set the paint bucket down in the farthest corner of the courtyard. It was pitch dark back there, so dark that they could hardly see each other. Daniel hoped that no one else could see them either.

Armin kneeled down, tried to open the paint bucket, couldn't. So he used a paintbrush handle to pry the lid up. But the wood of the handle splintered.

"Who rammed this lid down so hard?" he asked.

"You, of course," Daniel said.

Armin let his breath out, loud. Then, looking serious, he groped for his pocketknife, opened it, and stuck the blade under the lid.

"Even the paint is frozen stuck," Daniel observed.

"Quit griping," Armin said.

Finally he got the lid off. He wiped the white paint off the blade, snapped it shut, and pocketed the knife. Then he dipped a brush into the bucket, reached up high, and slapped a thick stroke onto the rough wall.

"Don't get the swastika backward again," Daniel said.

Armin didn't answer.

BATTLE

DANIEL ALSO TOOK UP A BRUSH. HE HADN'T painted his first stroke when he heard it once more. The sound of marching—still far off, but clearly audible.

He rested his brush on the bucket, stepped back a few paces, and listened.

"They're coming," he whispered.

Armin paused. "Who's coming where?"

"Just listen."

"I don't hear anything."

Armin went on painting. Daniel grunted and picked up his brush. He'd half finished the *R* for *Red Front, Go Croak* when he stopped again.

"They're coming I say!"

Armin calmly painted on.

Daniel listened awhile. The steps were getting louder, closer.

"Armin!" he said.

"You're scared shitless."

"And you're deaf. Can't you hear their boots?"

Armin sighed. "How'm I supposed to hear anything with you rattling on?"

They both held still and listened. From down on the Elbe came the *chug, chug* of passenger boats; from the Königstrasse, the rush of traffic. And in between, the sound of marchers' steps.

"They're far away," Armin said. "No reason to panic."

He resumed painting.

And the steps came nearer.

"Far away? They'll be here in a second." Daniel slapped the lid back on and picked up the paint bucket.

"Maybe they're ours," Armin said.

"Here, in this part of town?"

Armin moved forward, cupped his ear. "Yes, they're ours. I can tell by the sound of their steps."

"*Quatsch!* You cannot."

"Can so. The Red Front drags its feet. Give back the paint bucket."

That was when the marchers started singing:

> *"To battle! To battle!*
> *We were born to fight!*
> *We swore to Karl Liebknecht,*
> *And to Rosa Luxemburg,*
> *We'll battle for justice and right!"*

"You still think it's the SA?" asked Daniel.

"No. Red Front," Armin acknowledged.

"Let's get out of here!" Daniel grabbed the bucket and ran to the passageway, Armin one step behind.

The Red Front marchers were just on the other side of the wall.

Armin turned, ran back, climbed up, found a foothold from which he could see over the top.

"*Heh!* Get down!" Daniel called. What if a *Schupo* came by, or worse, more Communists?

But Armin leaned over the wall and yelled, "Red Front, go croak!"

"Will you *please* get down!" Daniel called.

Then all was quiet. A lamp came on in a window and cast a broad beam of light over the courtyard. The marchers halted and stopped singing.

One said, "Did you hear that?"

Daniel stood rooted in the passageway.

Armin gave no sign of jumping down. Instead, "Red Front, drop dead!" he yelled even louder. "We'll take revenge for Altona's Bloody Sunday!"

Daniel called, "Get down, idiot! Come on!"

"All right, I'm coming." Armin held on with just one hand and then leaped, but he landed left foot forward. He crumpled to his knees. "Shit!"

Meantime, they heard voices behind the wall muttering: "Never mind, that was just some little *Pimpf.*"

"All the same, let's have a look."

"Right, we're climbing over."

Armin examined his left ankle. Desperate, Daniel whispered, "Will you come on?"

"If I can—" Armin tried to pull himself up but could not stand on the sprained and bloodied ankle.

Just then two Communist faces peered over the wall. They didn't look much older than Armin and Daniel.

But when they swung themselves up top and started clambering down, Daniel saw that they were tough and strong and already had the muscular build of men.

"Look, a little Nazi rat," one said.

"Does your footie hurt?" the other taunted.

Armin tried limping away, but his ankle slowed him down.

Daniel still stood in the passageway, wanting to get out of there. But two of the Reds were jumping and rushing at Armin, who could hardly stand anymore! *I have to help him,* Daniel thought, and started toward his friend. He was scared, couldn't make himself go faster. Seeing the Reds with their fists out made Daniel hurry up. He saw Armin hurl himself at one of them and knock him to the ground. They rolled around, punching each other. And now a third Red came running, to make it three against one! Daniel ran also, as fast as he could now. But a shrill whistle sounded, stopping him in his tracks. . . . Police!

BLOOD BROTHERS

"THERE'S DIRT IN THIS SCRAPE," DANIEL SAID. "I'd better get it out."

He pushed Armin's face toward the barred window, from which only dim light came.

When Daniel touched the area where the skin on his ankle was raw, Armin shuddered and grabbed Daniel's wrist.

"Let go, or I can't clean it," Daniel said.

Armin let go, leaned back, clenched his teeth, and concentrated on a spot on the dark dirt floor.

They'd ended up in the Victoriastrasse police station. This would definitely earn them lasting fame, as Armin had hoped.

"All right, done," Daniel said, and stood up. "How could anybody be so stupid? We could have gotten away."

Armin pointed to his swollen ankle, then leaned back on the cot. "It just goes to show what Germany has come to," he muttered. "They didn't bother to arrest the Reds, oh, no."

"They got away," Daniel said.

The two of them fell silent. Daniel pictured tomorrow morning—what it would be like when a *Schupo* brought him home.

Armin groped in his pants pocket, pulled out a tobacco pouch, took a cigarette paper and rolled it between his fingers. He let the dry, dark brown tobacco trickle in and started rolling a smoke.

"But you don't have a light," said Daniel.

Armin winked. He stuck the cigarette in his mouth, leaned forward, reached into his shoe for a match, struck it against the shoe sole, and lit up.

Daniel looked to the barred door. "When the *Schupos* see that—"

"What'll they do? They've already booked us," Armin said.

He took a deep drag and offered the cigarette to Daniel. They took turns smoking and were quiet.

After a while Armin said, "My old man'll beat me to a pulp."

"Not mine; he never beats me," Daniel said. "He'll just keep quiet, never speak to me again."

"Lucky you," Armin said. "Mine never shuts up. He's been in a rotten mood ever since they took him off unemployment."

"They cut his insurance?"

"Right." Armin gave a bitter smile. "We're headed for the homeless shelter, to join the gang of 'antisocials' there. I'll be an 'antisocial' too."

They thought their own thoughts for a while. Daniel imagined his father not looking at him. For days. That was his way of punishing, ignoring Daniel completely, acting as though he didn't exist.

"Let's get some sleep," Daniel said.

"Good idea."

They lay down on the narrow cot. Daniel listened to the night sounds. The railroad tracks weren't far away. He heard the freight trains clatter by.

He thought Armin was sleeping. But, no, Armin sat up, cleared his throat, said, "I just wanted to thank you."

"What for?"

"You know. Before." Armin sat up straighter. "For not deserting me."

"Well, sure."

"You could have run away," Armin said. "I know lots of 'friends' who would have."

Daniel swung his legs to the ground.

"My friend screwed up. He got us into this. But even so," Daniel said with a shrug, "I couldn't leave him in the lurch."

"I'd do the same for you," said Armin, looking through the small window into the dark sky. "I call ours a real friendship. Yes . . ." He nodded thoughtfully. "That is something very rare."

Daniel looked out the window too. "Without friendship, nothing would be any good."

"Only men can be friends like this," Armin said. "Women can't. They don't even know what it is."

Daniel nodded, although he wasn't quite sure whether he agreed.

"We should seal it. Our friendship, I mean," Armin went on.

"Seal it, how?"

"Well, for instance, pledge blood brotherhood," Armin said.

"Fine with me," said Daniel.

"I mean, for real—slit our wrists open and all that. You know." Armin took hold of Daniel's wrist. "Here. Then we squeeze our wrists together."

"All right. Let's," Daniel said.

Armin stood up, muttering, "Too bad that *Schupo* took away my pocketknife."

"We could do it tomorrow," Daniel suggested.

"Uh-uh. Now."

Armin limped around the cell, bent over, searching. "There!" He found something: a sharp-edged, pointed stone.

"With that stone? It doesn't look too clean."

"So what?" Armin wiped it with his sleeve. Then he crouched on the cot and started working the stone against his wrist. He scraped away a few layers of skin. It hurt, but he tried not to show it.

They both inspected what he'd achieved.

"No blood's coming out," Armin said.

"Maybe we can pledge anyway," Daniel said.

"How do you mean?"

"Just press our wrists together."

"What good would that do?" Armin scoffed. "Why do you think they call it 'blood brotherhood'? Because you just press your wrists together?"

He got off the cot, went to the wall, kneeled down, and used the stone to scratch around in the dirt. "Look at that," he whispered. "You could do a first-class job of killing yourself with that."

Daniel went to him and saw the greenish glass. It shimmered in the weak light from the window.

Armin grasped it and ran the sharp edge against his thumb, testing.

"This'll work," he said, satisfied, and sat back on the cot.

Was he really going to slit his wrist open with this dirty piece of glass? You could catch all kinds of sicknesses that way, Daniel knew, from blood poisoning to tetanus. One of his mother's brothers had died of something like that as a child.

Armin held the piece of glass in his left hand, pressed his right wrist to the sharp edge, and, quickly, jerked his whole arm to the right, then, with a groan, raised the arm up high. Blood ran from the wrist to the elbow.

He pressed his hand to the wound and bent his upper body so his head hung between his knees.

"What's wrong?" Daniel asked.

"Nothing." Armin stood up suddenly. "Just wanted to see what's happening down there on the floor." He pulled his hand off the wound, wiped the blood on his pants, said, "Shit, this is really deep. Oh, well. It'll be all right."

He held out the piece of glass to Daniel. "Now you."

Daniel clenched his teeth and took it, rolled up his shirtsleeve, lowered his wrist to the sharp edge of the glass.

"Don't press too hard," said Armin.

"Obviously."

"Should I help you?"

"Nah."

Daniel took a breath. Then, eyes squeezed shut, he slid his wrist over the edge. The sharp pain went clear up to his nostrils.

But no blood came.

Daniel closed his eyes again and, leaning back, felt woozy from his gut upward.

"Thick skin," Armin said.

Daniel rested his wrist on the jagged edge of the glass, pressed down harder this time, jerked his arm to the side, then held it up. Thick drops of blood oozed from the cut.

"There, it worked. Good job!" said Armin. "All right, let's do the rest."

They sat across from each other and looked each other in the eyes.

"We hereby pledge blood brotherhood," Armin said.

"We hereby pledge blood brotherhood," said Daniel.

They leaned forward, arms touching. They pressed their wrists together crosswise and, with their free hands, covered the wrists thus joined. Daniel felt Armin's warm blood on his skin.

THE NEXT MORNING

IN THE KRAUSHAARS' LIVING ROOM THERE was a glassed-in alcove the family called their "winter garden." Sunlight streamed in—but no one seemed to notice it.

Sophie glanced at the pendulum clock that stood near the door. "It's strange that Daniel's not here yet," she said. She turned to her brother Sebastian and explained, "He spent the night at a friend's."

Sebastian nodded. "Yes. So you said."

Rheinhard Kraushaar contemplated the embroidery on the white tea-table cloth; Miriam, Sebastian's thirteen-year-old daughter, picked at the few cake crumbs left on her plate.

"Would you like another piece?" Sophie asked.

Miriam shook her head. "I'm full, thanks."

"You were starting to tell about Switzerland, Sophie," Sebastian said.

"Yes, what was it like?" Miriam asked.

"Oh, like a dream," Sophie said. "Wasn't it, Rheinhard?"

"Yes," said her husband in a toneless voice.

Sophie had been doing her best to keep up the conversation. She told how pleasant the weather had been and that they'd had a little accident on the drive back, but nothing serious.

The conversation halted. The only sound was the ticking of the clock.

So this is how it has to be when our family gathers, Sophie thought. She glanced at Rheinhard, wishing he'd say something. How could he behave like this?

Of course, if it had been up to him, Sebastian and Miriam's visit wouldn't have happened, especially not on a Sunday morning. "You know how precious my Sunday mornings are to me," he'd said when Sophie tried to prepare him for it.

"But they're passing through, and it's four years since we've had them to our house," Sophie said.

"Really, has it been that long?"

"Yes, and I'm starting to think it's silly that I have to meet my brother at the railroad-station restaurant every time he's in town."

"Oh, all right."

The welcome had gone smoothly enough. Rheinhard and Sebastian clapped each other on the shoulders, and Rheinhard acted pleasantly astonished, saying what an elegant young lady little Miriam had become since he'd seen her last.

But after that he'd excluded himself from the

conversation and only cleared his throat from time to time.

Adding to Sophie's discomfort, Daniel was still not home, and he'd sworn up and down that he'd be back no later than ten. She looked at the clock again—five minutes past twelve! She'd been providing small-talk topics for almost an hour, a task made all the harder by having to steer clear of any subject that could somehow lead to politics.

She looked around the table, hoping that someone would say something. No one did.

She called to the maid.

Maria's permanently blushing face appeared in the door.

"Yes, madam?"

"Would you bring us more tea, please," Sophie said.

Maria took the empty teapot and vanished.

Sophie sighed, straightened her back, and turned to Sebastian. "Will you be going to Munich on vacation, as you'd planned?"

"We're not taking a vacation this year," Sebastian answered. "So much work. Well, I suppose I should be glad I still have some."

Another silence followed. To Sophie's surprise, it was Rheinhard who came to the rescue. "Your business, Sebastian? It's all right, then?"

"When times are hard, people buy butter, not books," Sebastian replied. "With six million unemployed, people just don't have the money."

"The situation's improving, they say," Sophie said quickly. "So maybe you'll manage a vacation after all, when people start buying books again."

"But what kind of books, is the question. If Hitler becomes chancellor . . ." Sebastian left the sentence unfinished.

This was exactly the talk Sophie had tried to steer away from.

"Herr Marzahn said Hitler will never be chancellor," Miriam said.

"Who's Herr Marzahn?" Sophie asked.

"My teacher at school."

Rheinhard stopped staring out the window. "Your teacher is right," he said. "It won't happen."

"I wish I could believe that," Sebastian said. "But I can't. Not since his meeting with von Papen, our revered chancellor until recently. . . . No, I'm afraid we're in for a Hitler regime. All it needs is the presidential signature."

"Which it won't get," said Rheinhard, "because von Hindenburg will never allow that common rabble-rouser to be chancellor. You can count on it."

"It's true our field marshal and president mistrusts all but the highest-ranking officers," Sebastian said carefully. "But I saw the poor old fellow in a newsreel just last week. It was pathetic. Two lackeys had to prop him up. He's doddering; he's not himself anymore."

"Ah, well" was all Rheinhard could manage.

Sophie wished she could make her brother drop this topic. She sent him an imploring look.

But Sebastian was looking at Rheinhard and continued, "Von Hindenburg is senile, a circumstance our constitution did not foresee. Someone else will have to decide for him—his son, most likely. And he's not known for being anti-Nazi."

"The Nazis are the snows of yesteryear," Rheinhard said, dismissing Sebastian's worry. "They've been losing elections. Their party is bankrupt. If Strasser defects, the whole left wing will break away and, with it, the SA. We'll have a nationalistic government. Or a return to the monarchy."

Sebastian shook his head.

Rheinhard asked, "You have a better suggestion?"

Sebastian was silent. Finally he said, "The democrats and the Left still have the majority. But they aren't united. The only thing they agree on is saying no."

"My turn," Rheinhard said.

But Maria came in with the teapot just then, providing the needed interruption, and so the storm was averted . . . for the moment. "Enough of politics," Sophie said. "Who'd like a little more tea?"

She refilled Sebastian's and Rheinhard's cups. She checked the clock again and said, "What a pity Daniel's not here. Miriam, you must find us grownups very boring."

Miriam nodded.

Rheinhard turned to her and asked, "How are things at school?"

"Pretty good," she answered.

"School—that's another problem," Sebastian said. "The HJ boys want the schoolyard *judenfrei*, so now they have little pogroms during recess."

"Just childish pranks," Rheinhard said.

Sebastian looked him squarely in the eyes. "I think you have no idea what's really happening in this country. You know what I've been considering seriously these last few months? Whether Miriam and I shouldn't emigrate."

"Maybe to Brussels, to Aunt Martha," Miriam said.

"But what would you live on, in Brussels?" Sophie asked. "You could hardly start a German bookstore there."

"I know," Sebastian said.

Another pause. Then Rheinhard spoke, a bit too loudly. "So you're thinking of running away from your problems again?"

Sophie looked appalled.

"I've never run away from problems," Sebastian replied.

How can I defuse this? Sophie wondered frantically.

"Who, exactly, ran away back then?" Sebastian persisted.

"I know where *I* was," Rheinhard said. "Exactly where I belonged."

Sebastian leaned forward and said, "It's a puzzle to me how you can still believe that story, even after fifteen years. You were the one to hide from reality. You escaped. You fled to the front because you didn't want to look the truth in the eye."

Now here it was, the most dreaded subject. After all her trying to avoid it, Sophie, in an odd, bitter way, was almost glad.

Rheinhard leaned back. Head slightly lowered, he stared out the window again. This way he avoided Sophie's eyes.

Nonetheless, she could see he was trying to control himself.

He put his hand on the table and said, "Let's not talk about it."

"We'd lost the war!" Sebastian went on.

"Let's not talk about it," Rheinhard repeated.

"But you kept it going," Sebastian said. "Against our own people."

"*Who* waged war against our own people?" Rheinhard burst out. "There's only one word in the German language for what *you* did back then: treason."

Sebastian didn't answer. His gaze swept over the room and came to rest on Miriam. "It might be better if we left," he said.

First he, then Miriam stood up.

Speechless, Sophie rose and stood facing her brother. "Your train doesn't leave until two," she said, much too quietly.

Sebastian nodded, hesitated for a moment, but went to get their coats.

Sophie followed them into the foyer. "All the same, it was good to see you both," she said.

"And you," Sebastian said.

Miriam had put her coat on. "I can't find my scarf," she said.

They searched through the closet.

Then Miriam found it in her coat pocket.

They said good-bye quickly, voices low.

Returning to the living room, Sophie glanced at Rheinhard but said nothing.

He had the newspaper in his hand but didn't open it. He returned Sophie's gaze and said, "I'm sorry. I didn't want that."

Sophie cleared away the tea things and carried them down to the kitchen herself, rather than call Maria, who would be busy preparing the midday meal.

When Sophie returned, she stepped into the glassed-in alcove and looked out at the garden, at the little hawthorn tree with its delicate thorns visible only in winter once it had lost its foliage.

After a moment Rheinhard opened up the newspaper and started reading.

Sophie turned to her husband and said, "I knew it would end the way it did."

Rheinhard let the paper drop, started to put it carefully back together, and asked, "Why did he have to come here?"

Sophie didn't answer.

"It's he who can't accept me," Rheinhard said.

"It's mutual," said Sophie.

"No. I acknowledge that we hold different opinions, but I can accept him. I don't let myself be ruled by my emotions."

Sophie pondered this last sentence and could not think how to reply. Then the front doorbell rang.

Moments later, when Sophie opened the door, she saw at first only the rotund, friendly-seeming face of the *Schupo* in his uniform.

"Frau Kraushaar?" he asked, sounding ill at ease.

She nodded, and suddenly she was overcome with immeasurable fear for her son. "W-Where is—?" she stuttered.

Not till the policeman nodded his head and she'd opened the door wider did she see Daniel, dressed in shabby clothing, much too big on him. And why that bandage wrapped around his wrist?

"Good morning, Mutti," Daniel said to her. His face was streaked with dirt. "Sorry I'm late."

ARMIN'S SUNDAY

AT RECESS MONDAY MORNING ARMIN AND Daniel were the only topic of conversation. Every student in the Christianeum knew that they had spent a night in jail. Even Manfred Maas, who was in the next-to-highest class and already a troop leader in the HJ, condescended to ask them about it.

During second recess they were called to Herr Direktor Doktor Kammacher's office and had to sit through a long, earnest warning: It could not be tolerated that students of this *Gymnasium* disport themselves in courtyards and back alleys by night, and so on and so forth. But when he'd finished lecturing, he clapped them on the shoulders, winked, and said, "You boys know how it is: Do what you like, just don't get caught."

After school Armin and Daniel crossed the Mühlenstrasse and strolled along the wide, tree-lined Palmaille. This route was out of the way for them both, but they were in no hurry to get home.

Armin reported how he'd fared after their night in

the cell: A *Schupo* brought him home, the same as Daniel. "Of course I told him I was capable of finding my own way. But he insisted, said it was his duty to hand me over personally. 'Doesn't our police force have more important things to do?' I asked." Armin shook his head.

They came to the Altona Balkon, a small square on the bank of the Elbe, sat on a bench there, and Armin continued:

"So I slogged along beside the *Schupo* all the way down the Königstrasse, imagining what was ahead, not looking forward to it, you can bet. When we turned into our street, I told him one more time that I could definitely find my own way. But he didn't listen.

"When we got there, my old man was already down in the courtyard, waiting. The *Schupo* gave a blow-by-blow account of my misdeeds. Meantime, a few neighbors came down and stood around gaping at me. My old man kept quiet—no sermon, no harangue.

"He looked under the bandage the *Schupo*'d put around my wrist. Then he just kind of slumped down, sat there all tuckered out, still not saying anything, even after the *Schupo* left. He should at least have yelled at me! I started feeling bad. I mean, I know he's an old Social Democrat and what it means to him that I, his son, and so on, blah, blah, blah.

"He took out his handkerchief and blew his nose,

loud. Then—as if he'd suddenly made up his mind—he grabbed me by the arm, by the bandage even, and dragged me into the cellar. He locked me in and left me there. I knew where he was going. I also knew we had only a few mark left that had to last us the whole week. But his favorite beer joint opens early on Sunday.

"I sat in the dark cellar and thought about that, and I started to hate him. I mean, really hate him. Hanging out in bars, guzzling beer, and yammering like a washerwoman—that's all he knows how to do.

"After about an hour I heard his voice out in the courtyard. He'd drunk his beer; now he was ready to go look in Mother's cooking pot, see what's for midday dinner. I figured he might come get me. But he went upstairs, not down.

"I thought, 'Maybe after he's eaten.' But, no, he'd forgotten me.

"I was down there the whole day. Man, it was cold. And black as night. Well, you get used to freezing and the dark, but not to starving. . . . I hadn't had breakfast, remember. I was getting hungrier and hungrier.

"It felt like I hadn't eaten in a year. It got so bad, I took down one of my mother's jars from the shelf. I knew, of course, that was strictly *verboten*.

"It was roast goose! We only have it once a year, at Christmas. She always makes preserves of every bit left over. And it gets saved for big occasions, like Easter or Grampa's birthday. But I was so starved, I polished off the whole jar, including the nice goose fat at the bottom.

"I'd just finished when the cellar door was pulled open. My mother, coming to get me. She snatched the jar out of my hands and scolded and screamed and dragged me to my feet.

"When we got upstairs, she shoved the jar in my father's face, like that was the last straw! So then he started bellowing, and he heaved me into the hall, pulled his belt out of his pants, and beat me. But the belt didn't do a good enough job. So he took a hand broom. And I was so sick from the goose fat, I thought I'd throw up."

Armin laughed bitterly.

"My mother tried to pull at me from behind, but my old man wouldn't let up. He kept beating me with that wooden thing, on my back, my head, my arm. . . . Then the handle broke off.

"My father just stood there. My mother started bawling, 'Now the hand broom's busted too! And we don't have any money. How'm I supposed to sweep up and keep this place clean?' . . . That's when my father got all blue in the face.

"'Lie down,' my mother yelled, 'lie down. It's your heart!' My father's knees were shaking; he had to hold on to the doorframe. And my mother was screaming about what I'd done, and couldn't I see what I was doing to my father, and about how we had no money, and now the goose was gone, and the hand broom busted, but maybe the broom maker could fix it. . . .

"I wasn't listening. I felt sick as a dog from the goose fat, ran to the toilet, and threw up."

FAMILY COURT

THE TWO FRIENDS SAT FOR A WHILE AND watched the fishing boats casting off from their moorings.

Finally Armin asked, "So, how was it at your house?"

"What?"

"The return of the prodigal son."

Daniel thought, *How should I tell it?* What went on at Armin's was often comical, or brutal, like yesterday, but at least things *happened*: The mother yelled, the father beat him up or almost had a heart attack—things you could make into a story. At Daniel's house it was nothing like that. And, supposedly, no punishment was given.

"How was it? The usual. Family court in session."

"And?"

"My father as prosecutor and judge, my mother as defense attorney. Painting slogans on a wall, getting arrested—those were *not* my worst offense. No, it was that I'd done it behind their backs . . . and in bad company—"

"With that dirty proletarian, me?"

"Right. I was supposed to decide what my punishment should be. As usual. I said, 'No allowance for a week.'

"My father hit the ceiling. 'You obviously don't realize the seriousness of your offense. The punishment must be commensurate with the deed. In this case, the accused had best forgo his friendship with that'—he called you a 'working-class roughneck.' Sorry.

"Then my mother pleaded sternly: 'Young man, you've always been ready to accept responsibility for your actions. Now you must understand that continued contact with that badly-brought-up ruffian is only doing you harm.'

"'Objection, Your Honors,' I said. 'That badly-brought-up ruffian attends the Christianeum, just as I do.'

"'Nonetheless, I'm disappointed,' the prosecutor said. 'I'd expected my son to be capable of proposing an appropriate punishment. True, mature morality requires that one accept the consequences of one's actions . . .' And so on."

Daniel looked up. From where they sat, they had a view over the wide river to the marshlands beyond, all the way to the Harburger Mountains.

"So, what was the verdict?" Armin asked.

"Guilty. Room arrest. Until and including next Sunday."

"Well, that's not so bad."

Armin never understood what was so bad about the rituals at the Kraushaars'. He couldn't imagine how it felt, sitting at supper with one's parents for exactly forty-five minutes every evening, and in all that time not once being looked at or spoken to.

Armin checked his wound, now covered by a neat pink scar. He grinned and said, "All in all, wasn't it fabulous?"

"Yes," Daniel agreed.

"And what'll we do today?" Armin asked.

"Nothing. I'm grounded, remember? I'd better get home."

"I could visit," Armin said. "Your father won't be there. And your mother's not like that, is she?"

Daniel's face brightened a little. "I don't know if she'll let you in, but if you want to try . . ."

"Sure I do," Armin said. "I can't let you stew in your room all by yourself. We could go on with the Battle of the Somme."

ONSLAUGHT IN PAPIER-MÂCHÉ

THE BIG PLATFORM ON WOODEN BLOCKS took up half of Daniel's room. On it was a papier-mâché landscape carefully constructed, with attention to topography and geographical details.

Daniel got the lead soldiers out of the drawer. He had personally cast them and painted their uniforms.

Armin switched on the radio and turned the dial, hoping for a symphony as background to their game. He wished *he* had a radio in his room. But there was no chance of that. His parents didn't even have one.

He tuned in Radio Deutschland, as usual, but it had a political discussion on. The station next to it was broadcasting an opera, not exactly the ideal accompaniment. Farther down the dial, though, he found what he was looking for.

"That sounds like Bruckner," Daniel said.

Armin shrugged. He could tell what made good background, but he didn't know a thing about classical music. Daniel, on the other hand, had to go to concerts with his parents every other Sunday and could reel off the entire repertoire.

Armin stood at the platform. From the radio came a soft, yet tension-filled adagio. He gazed into the distance, then at the landscape, and pointed at the thin blue river flowing through the plain. "September 1916. We are at the western front," he announced in a calm, firm voice. "French forces have broken through at the Somme. . . ." He motioned to Daniel to bring reinforcements, then poked his fingers into the papier-mâché.

"*Heh*, what are you doing?" Daniel shouted.

"The Germans are digging feverishly through the night. They need more, deeper trenches," Armin explained.

Daniel brought up more gray-clad German infantry.

Armin placed the French artillery in position: grenade launchers and cannons with springs inside them that could fire little cannonballs.

"It's daybreak," he announced. "The heavy barrage of enemy fire is about to resume."

Daniel fired the cannons and made noises of grenades exploding.

"The earth is trembling under the assault," Armin intoned. "Our troops have no other recourse than to burrow down into the still unfinished trenches." He scrunched the slightly-too-big soldiers as deep into the indentations as he could.

Meanwhile, Daniel grabbed a plane and circled it over the battlefield. "Enemy aircraft sighted! Ten, fifteen propeller planes! Double-deckers! They're scouting out our positions. We know what that means: deadlier bombardment, because more accurately aimed."

Armin took over: "Grenades are exploding directly in front of the German trenches, wreaking havoc, causing shrapnel storms. But our valiant soldiers in field gray will not retreat. Each time the enemy fire abates, they look up over the trenches and shoot off salvo after salvo at the French."

Daniel made a few French soldiers teeter and keel over.

Armin raised his arms, extended them like a maestro over the entire landscape. As the radio music surged to a crescendo and subsided, he declared: "All is still. The artillery rests. . . ."

Again he gazed into the distance. And as though by magic, a soft, almost playful melody began.

"The stillness is deceptive," Armin said earnestly. "Over on the French side there is stirring." The radio obliged with ominous trumpet blasts. "Figures steal through the underbrush. They're coming nearer, storming forward in formation; they've almost reached our outermost trenches."

Hectically, he and Daniel set French soldiers by the handful down in the open field directly in front of the German positions, while on the radio the first movement of the symphony strove toward its climax.

"The right flank," Daniel exclaimed. "They're about to capture our right flank! Our brave German infantry defend themselves with all their might. Bayonets at the ready, they hurl themselves into the battle, man for man!"

Armin moved in more and more French soldiers, including many who'd already been shot. "Artillery!" he shouted. "We need artillery up here, so we can shoot at the French who're breaking through!"

"Grenade launchers on their way!" Daniel rushed to the closet and brought out a whole cartonful. "But the ground is deep in mud. Horses and men make desperate efforts to pull them through. At last they're ready! Fire!"

Again Arnim took over: "Grenades rain down upon the advancing French. Entire battalions are getting blasted straight into the air. Only the dead and the severely wounded are landing near our trenches."

"They're in retreat! They're flooding back. They have suffered tremendous losses," Daniel reported breathlessly while knocking down French soldiers row by row. "We have withstood their onslaught, demolished their attack."

Armin, standing tall, swept his glance over the ravaged landscape. From the radio came soft and lyrical sounds again. "Calm is restored," he said, pushing a strand of hair back from his face. "Dusk slowly settles over the blood-drenched battlefield. How many noble German men have fallen for the Fatherland today? But they gave their lives gladly. And their deaths were not in vain. Because they died for us all."

Daniel sank into his armchair. "My father had a button shot off his uniform in that battle," he said. "Just like that. . . . It was a ricochet."

"Those are the most dangerous kind," Armin said, his eyes still on the battlefield. "Four hundred or more years from now people will still be talking about how brave those German soldiers were, don't you think, Daniel?"

VICTORY PARADE

THEN CAME THE NEWS BULLETIN.

They were just sorting the soldiers, putting them back into their right places in the drawer. Bruckner's Fifth Symphony was still playing. Suddenly the music stopped. The broadcast was interrupted.

Armin turned up the volume. And they heard the voice of a newscaster: "Reich President von Hindenburg has appointed Adolf Hitler, leader of the National Socialist Party, chancellor of the Reich."

It was January 30, 1933.

Armin and Daniel stood looking at each other. They could scarcely believe it. Daniel could feel how his eyes were glowing.

He glanced at the ravaged papier-mâché landscape. Suddenly he felt ashamed. They'd thrown themselves into the game like little children. Now, in this moment, Daniel knew that the time of toy soldiers was over. In this moment he and Armin had grown too old for such childish pastimes.

They ran out into the street, just as they were,

without jackets on. Yes, Daniel was grounded. But that didn't matter now. His mother was talking anxiously on the telephone and didn't even notice that he'd left.

The street and sidewalks were covered with leaflets. "Hitler is chancellor of the Reich!" Paperboys shouted the news as they handed out special editions.

It was icy cold, but Daniel and Armin didn't feel it. They ran to the Altona *S-Bahn* station, where SA men were distributing leaflets about a victory parade through the inner city starting soon.

The boys jumped onto the next train, rode to the inner city, got off at the central railroad station, hurried up the Mönckebergstrasse, and were almost at the market square in front of the Hamburg town hall when they saw the fire.

It was already dark. SA men hoisted torches and sang the Horst Wessel song: "Raise high the flag, close tight the ranks . . ."

Their footsteps thundered to the beat, seeming to shatter the pavement.

Armin and Daniel stood arm in arm and sang along from deep in their throats. They stared at the parade, at its red flags with black swastikas, and at the SA men's fierce, determined faces in the torches' glare.

Then came the HJ divisions. Endless columns, as resolute as the SA but with something high and holy

shining from their eyes. They were children, after all.
And they sang:

"Raise high the flag, close tight the ranks,
SA, march on, with firm and steadfast tread.
Our comrades killed in Red Front confrontations
March in their spirits side by side with us!

Stand back, here come the brown battalions!
Make room for the brave men of the SA!
Be ready! A new day is dawning
Of freedom and of bread!"

Daniel would have loved to join them, to march
along. Those HJ boys weren't much older than he;
some were even younger. But their faces were so
earnest, so dedicated, it made him feel ashamed. He
asked himself, *Who am I, anyway?*

His life seemed laughable to him. He played with
lead soldiers on a landscape of papier-mâché. And on
weekends he went for walks with Mama and Papa.
Everybody treated him like a little boy. When important things were going on, people said, "You can't
understand that. It has nothing to do with you."

But those boys in uniform, with their belts and
buckles—some had knives in leather holsters—they
were doing something important, not frittering their
time away.

They sang of comrades shot in battles—real ones, not papier-mâché. Their minds were on life-and-death matters, not on soccer games or supper. Daniel ached to belong and to be as committed as they to a cause of highest importance: the future of Germany.

He decided to join the HJ. His parents couldn't forbid it anymore.

UNSIGNED

SOPHIE DIDN'T WONDER WHY RHEINHARD had come home for the midday meal twice in a row. It wasn't unusual. He often came home if he happened to be in Altona, at a trial or some other business, often without letting her know in advance. What struck her as unusual, however, was that he seemed in no hurry to get back to the office after dessert. She *did* wonder about that.

Today, even after Daniel left for soccer practice, Rheinhard was still sitting there. He reached into his inner jacket pocket, took out an envelope, and laid it on the table. Then he stood up and went into the library.

He hadn't said a word. But Sophie knew his ways, she understood: He meant that she could read this letter, if she wanted to.

She picked up the envelope. It had no return address. Inside were two sheets of paper with typing on both sides.

Honored Fellow German, it began.

With this letter, the new reality in Germany—it had begun on January 30, now two months past—burst in on the Kraushaars and caused the first upheaval in their lives.

Some things, of course, had been noticeably different since Hitler had seized power. Still, Rheinhard and Sophie, like so many other people, had not taken the new regime too seriously. In past years there'd been so many governmental changes, they'd grown accustomed to cabinets switching, ministers coming and going. Why worry that this vulgar demagogue from nowhere would last for long?

But so far he'd held on. And more than that. In February, the Reichstag, seat of the parliament, burned down. In March, Hitler's "Empowerment Law" made him dictator over Germany, not merely chancellor.

Then began what the Nazis called *Gleichschaltung*, "equalization"—a harmless-sounding word for the ruthless process of stamping out all opposition. In Altona, only a few hundred meters from the Kraushaars' house, SA men occupied the town hall. The head of the local Nazi party appointed himself mayor and had the senators taken into "protective custody." This was clearly not done for their protection. The former mayor, Max Brauer, had to flee like a common criminal. The SA took up a collection for gallows from which to hang him. And no one grasped that now they were defenseless against the new authorities.

One time Sophie witnessed a rather comical scene: SA men pulled the old black, red, and gold flag down from the town hall. They tried to set it on fire but didn't have enough gasoline.

Probably, she thought, the thick material was damp. It just wouldn't burn. The SA leader screamed with rage. A crowd had gathered, and some people were laughing. Many more matches were struck, but only one tiny burn hole resulted. Finally the leader crumpled the flag into a ball, threw it to one of his men, and shouted, "Shove it in the oven when you get home!"

This scene took place on the Square of the Republic, newly renamed "Adolf Hitler Square."

And now here was this letter. She put it in front of her on the table and, reading it, felt something tightening inside her.

It wasn't really a letter, but a circular, unsigned. It told about a Socialist Democrat journalist from Lübeck, Dr. Nolmitz—a friend of Sebastian's. Sophie had met him once or twice. He'd been arrested and was sent to Fuhlsbüttel, a prison to the north of Hamburg with a newly established special unit for political detainees. There he was tortured, beaten on the head till his scalp burst open and blood spurted to the ceiling. When he fainted, they brought him back to consciousness by kicking him in the scrotum, then made him run and chased him through the corridors.

Sophie pushed the circular away, then drew it near and forced herself to read on.

It said that Nolmitz had tried several times to get himself killed by standing at the window behind the beds in the group cell. This was strictly forbidden, and the guards had orders to shoot whoever did it. The reason he failed was that his cell mates feared he would endanger them as well, and so they always pulled him back.

Nolmitz was put in solitary and underwent more torture. He wrote all of it down, on cigarette papers. In the end he hanged himself. But he'd hidden the cigarette papers under the lid of his pocket watch, which, after he died, was returned to his wife.

All the time she was reading, Sophie thought of Sebastian. He, too, was a known socialist. Was he now facing imprisonment? She shivered uncontrollably.

THE BOOKS

SOPHIE REMEMBERED HAVING READ ABOUT the opening of the special unit at Fuhlsbüttel. The newspaper article described it as a kind of rest cure for political extremists. Of course she hadn't believed that, but neither had she tried to imagine what really went on in such a place. She folded the circular and put it back in the envelope.

In a little while she called Maria and told her to clear away the dishes from the midday meal. Then she went to the library, stopped at the door, and asked, "Rheinhard, where did that circular come from?"

Her husband had his reading glasses on and stood scrutinizing the bookcase. "The circular? Anonymous," he answered. "It arrived in this morning's mail and wasn't sent to only me, but to many lawyers."

"And what do you plan to do?"

Rheinhard was pulling books down off the shelves. "It's a dilemma," he said, turning to her. "If I bring it to the police, it will get me into difficulties. They'll ask who sent it. If I don't give them a name—

which I cannot do—they perhaps will put me in jail. But if I don't bring it to them, I place myself under suspicion."

Sophie entered the room. "Shouldn't one pass this circular around to other people, not just to lawyers?" she asked.

Rheinhard pressed his lips together and shook his head. "Absolutely not." He carried the books he'd removed to a side table and set them down. "Besides, that whole business is exaggerated," he said. "Abusing prison inmates is nothing new; it always happens, in other countries, too. Germany is in the midst of a revolution. And that sort of thing never ends entirely without bloodshed."

Sophie went toward him. "You call this a revolution? I say it's a return to barbarism!"

Rheinhard didn't answer.

Sophie started looking through the books he'd taken from the shelves. "Why are you rearranging our library?" she asked.

"I'm not rearranging it."

"What then?"

"Sophie, I've decided: I'll bring in the circular."

"What has that to do with these books?"

"When I bring the circular to the police, it's likely there will be a house search."

"Yes, and?"

Rheinhard just threw up his hands.

She studied the spines of the books. "You mean we have something to hide? As far as I know, we don't have anything subversive that's a danger to the state."

She read the authors' names: Heinrich Heine, Arthur Schnitzler, Stefan Zweig . . . "Why these?"

"Isn't it obvious?" Rheinhard said.

"You mean because they're Jewish?"

He nodded. "I'll just put them in the attic for a while."

Sophie paced the room. Then she picked up Heine's *Buch der Lieder*. It was an old Insel Verlag edition she'd inherited from her parents. The red color was coming off its velvety cover and stuck to her hands.

"Why take Heine up to the attic?" she asked. "Why not take Goethe and Schiller, too? Didn't you just say that you don't think things are so bad? What's wrong with Heine? He's a German poet, after all."

"As I was just trying to explain to you, this circular can land me in the devil's own kitchen."

"But reading Heine and these others is not forbidden, is it?"

"Not in so many words."

"What will happen if they find this book by Heine here?"

"Maybe it will give them the pretext they're waiting for. I'm one of the best-known lawyers in Hamburg."

"Yes, and? Wouldn't that just make it harder for them to cause you difficulties?"

"I'm married to a woman of Jewish ancestry." Rheinhard gathered up the books, started to leave the room, then turned around and faced her, saying, "We'll manage for a few months without these."

Just then the doorbell rang.

The sound gave Sophie a jolt. Rheinhard, too. They looked toward the foyer, then at each other. Neither of them said it aloud, but both had the same thought.

Rheinhard put down the stack of books, straightened up, went to the hall, and opened the door.

"Oh, it's you!"

"Who else?"

Sophie sighed with relief, hearing Daniel's voice.

He ran through the hall and threw the bag with his sweaty soccer clothes on the cellar steps. His face was still flushed from practice, maybe from excitement, too.

He followed his father to the living room. He hesitated a moment. Then he took a slip of paper out of his shirt pocket and laid it on the table.

THE APPLICATION

"VATI?"

"Yes?"

"Can you . . . can you sign this?"

Rheinhard went to the table and bent over the slip of paper. It was a form.

"What's this for?"

"You have to sign it," Daniel said.

Rheinhard looked it over. There was an *X* at the bottom, where the parent was to sign. It was an application to the HJ. He drew his eyebrows together.

Daniel looked his father in the face. "Everyone is joining," he said. "All my friends. Armin, too."

Rheinhard turned around and called, "Sophie? Kindly come here."

"In a moment," Sophie answered from the library. "What's going on?"

"I want to show you something," Rheinhard said. She came.

"Have a look at this." Rheinhard handed her the form. She read it through calmly. Then she turned to Daniel.

Daniel stood very straight and looked his parents in the eyes. "Everyone is joining. Really."

"Yes?" Sophie asked.

"There is no law that says you always must do what everyone else is doing," Rheinhard said.

"I don't, always," Daniel said.

"You haven't found the right friends," Sophie said. "If you want to join a youth group, then let's think about it. There are many you would like, the Pathfinders, for instance."

I knew she'd start in with something like that, Daniel thought. "I don't want to join the Pathfinders," he said. "I want—"

Rheinhard cut him off. "You're being rude."

Daniel swallowed and tried a new approach. "Listen to me, please. The HJ isn't like the SA. It's basically not so different from the Pathfinders. They go on hikes, they sing folk songs—"

"You needn't tell us what the Hitler Jugend is," Rheinhard said with a bitter smile.

"We have nothing against hiking or folk songs," Sophie added. "You know that."

"I *don't* know that! I can't understand what you're so worried about. It is an honor to be in the HJ. And you can't forbid it. You're not allowed to."

Rheinhard looked at him searchingly. "Since when do you tell your parents what we're allowed and not allowed to do?"

"I'll still apply, even if you don't sign this form."

"I certainly will not sign it," Rheinhard said. He folded up the form and waved his hand dismissively, as though the problem were resolved, end of discussion.

"You can't forbid it," Daniel repeated.

"Come on, let's—," Sophie began.

But Rheinhard broke in. "Enough of this! Lately we've had to be grateful if our estimable son favors us by showing up for supper. At school things are going downhill too, Daniel, since you've been spending so much time with that Armin, and all you think about is soccer. This will have to stop. You are grounded for today. And no supper."

"Vati . . ." Daniel clenched his jaw, trying to hold back the tears that were gathering in his eyes.

"Oh, dear, will our young hero now start crying?" his father asked. "The same boy who is so eager to join the new Germany's elite, hard-as-steel-and-iron Hitler Jugend?"

"No, Rheinhard," Sophie said. "Not like that. We have to talk about it. Together."

"What is there to talk about?"

"Maybe we should tell him."

"Tell him what? There's nothing to tell."

"Others, unfortunately, don't agree with you, Rheinhard."

"If you tell him, you'll be doing just what those fanatics want you to."

Daniel was baffled. What was all this about?

THE GRANDPARENTS

RHEINHARD HAD TURNED AWAY. SOPHIE looked at Daniel. Her mouth was closed tight, as though she wanted never to speak another word.

But then she did: "Daniel . . . we haven't talked about it with you until now because we thought it wouldn't matter."

Could I have been adopted? was the first thing that came into Daniel's mind. *But that wouldn't have anything to do with the application form. So what was it?*

"But there are people for whom it matters a great deal," Sophie went on. "And, unfortunately, what they say is what counts in Germany today."

"What are you talking about?" Daniel asked.

"Well, you see . . ." Sophie paused, cleared her throat. "It's not so easy to explain: My parents, your grandparents, whom you hardly knew, were—no, they really weren't Jewish, they'd resigned from the Jewish Community, withdrawn their names from its registry when they were young. They wanted to be Germans, first and foremost. Not Jewish in the old ways, keeping kosher and all that—"

"Jewish?" Daniel was stunned; he couldn't believe it.

"They were Germans, of course," Sophie went on. "But they both came from Jewish families. They withdrew from the Jewish Community because they were nonobservant. I was brought up like every other German girl. We celebrated Christmas, we had a tree, and we sang Christmas songs. For a long time I didn't even know that I was of Jewish descent. . . . But by the Nazi definition, I am a Jewess now. I would never describe myself as such. That makes no difference to them. And by their definition, you are half Jewish, non-Aryan."

"Me?"

"Yes. Maybe now you'll understand; that is why you can't join the Hitler Jugend."

Daniel couldn't understand her at all. The words buzzed in his ears. He could almost not hear her. What was it she was saying? "You're a Jewess?" he asked.

"It's the crazy Nazis who want to make me into one," Sophie said. "I'm German."

"Why didn't you tell me?" Daniel asked.

"Because it didn't mean anything to us. I never thought about it."

Sophie raised her hands, as though she wanted to say, *It hardly mattered to me.* But she didn't, seeing how devastated Daniel looked.

He stared at the floor. He couldn't think clearly anymore. Then he burst out, "How could you keep something like that from me? I'm not . . . I'm not, I can't be, you know, what you just said."

"Half Jewish?"

"I don't want anything to do with that! I'm a German, like everyone else."

"Naturally. I can see that. But—"

"It's not a matter of what you want, Daniel," his father broke in. "It's not we who invented this claptrap about races. The Nazis, whom you so admire, have given us that. You will have to come to terms with it and take the consequences."

Daniel looked at his father. "Why did you do it?" he asked. "Why did you marry a Jewess?"

Rheinhard stared at him. "Why did I *what*?"

"That's why I'm half Jewish now," Daniel said. "Because you married a Jewess."

Rheinhard didn't answer. He gave Daniel a look that hurt more than the smack in the face he gave him next.

Sophie stepped between them. "Rheinhard!"

He pushed her aside and stared at Daniel. Daniel's knees were shaking.

"Leave," his father said. "You are grounded till Monday morning. Go on. Out!"

Sophie wanted to run after him, to comfort him, but sat down. Rheinhard rubbed the hand with which he'd smacked Daniel.

They were silent. Sophie started to cry. "It's getting worse and worse," she said softly, "and it'll get worse still."

"He'll calm down," said Rheinhard.

"How can this go on?" she asked, not looking at her husband. "If this regime stays in power, what'll happen?"

Rheinhard stood behind her and put his hands on her shoulders. "I know, it's terrible," he said. "But it will soon be over. You'll see. The mischief will stop as suddenly as it began."

Sophie thought of Daniel. What was he doing, alone in his room?

She could understand how he'd reacted. She even managed not to feel offended. But afraid, yes.

She was terrified, more with every moment she spent here with Rheinhard while Daniel was alone in his room.

She could feel how her son, at this very moment, would be distancing himself from her. What he needed was a strong, self-confident mother. A mother who was there and who, when he pulled away from her, would still be there. She wished she were that strong, but she questioned it.

"It wasn't right, sending him upstairs," she said.

"At some time I, too, will have to take the consequences," Rheinhard said. "It's senseless talking with him. Daniel needs a bit more clarity in his life. He has to know what to expect from me. At best, and also at worst."

"I'm afraid we'll lose him," Sophie said.

VOLCANOES

DANIEL LAY ON HIS BED, STARING OVER AT the bookshelf. Lined up on top stood a few of his favorite lead soldiers. But he didn't really see them, nor the books behind them. He felt trapped inside an awful dream. Everything was wrong. And he knew this dream would not end, there'd be no waking up. All right, then, he'd just lie here. For all eternity. That was the only thing to do: He decided he'd never leave his room again.

Sounds from downstairs drifted up: his mother starting to cry; his father speaking in a deep, consoling voice; then his mother again. But Daniel could make out only a word or two, a fragment of a sentence here and there.

Listening to his mother crying, he tried to steel himself against her. He told himself her tears were forced. *Cry all you want,* he thought, *but it's no use. You're a Jewess. The Nazis will stay in power. And the "mischief" won't be over soon.*

After a while it grew quiet down there.

Daniel stayed on his bed and looked out the window at the first stars appearing in the blue-black sky. He got annoyed at the twigs of the tree for blocking his view, so he couldn't recognize the constellations. . . .

He lay there for about an hour, trying to forget the scene with his parents. He still felt caught, but he started thinking this bad dream *could* end.

After all, he was only *half* Jewish. He'd heard that the Führer sometimes made exceptions and personally granted honorary Aryan status to certain selected half-Jews. Then they could be officers or join the SS. Of course, for this to happen, Daniel would have to leave home, disown his mother—which seemed not so terrible when he pictured himself standing before the Führer, the Führer pinning a decoration on his chest, clapping him on the shoulder: *There, now you're an Aryan.* Then he could join the HJ and be an officer in the Wehrmacht when he grew up.

He imagined moving to Berlin. He'd know his way around, because he'd already been there several times. . . . After a while he felt bored. He looked out the window again, and got madder and madder at that damned tree.

He thought about volcanoes, Mount Krakatoa erupting in Indonesia. His father had given him a book about that.

He sprang up, fetched the book from his desk, threw himself back on the bed, and read.

What an eruption that was, back in 1883, the biggest of any volcano, ever! It hurled a huge chunk of the earth's crust straight up into the air. The blast was heard as far away as Australia, and even South America. It made a tidal wave thirty meters high that went clear around the globe and took thirty-six thousand lives. And the vast amount of rock and earth that got flung into the atmosphere caused three years of glowing sunsets everywhere in the world.

Daniel imagined going on an expedition with Armin. Someday they'd explore Mount Krakatoa, the two of them. . . . And, slowly, he felt better.

I MANEUVERED THE JEEP PAST RUTS AND RUBBLE along the former Königstrasse. Just before the burned-out Altona town hall, I veered to the left, drove a hundred meters farther, then stopped between two great maple trees and got out.

Butterflies fluttered; the air smelled of spring. I crossed through a stretch of straggly grass and reached the small, pebble-strewn Altona Balkon.

We'd often sat in this square, Armin and I. Now there were no more benches. Probably, people had chopped them up and used them for firewood.

I leaned against the wrought-iron railing and looked down the steep slope to the Elbe. The incoming tide dragged sluggish, gray water upstream. There were no ships to be seen. The Hamburg port had been closed for many months.

This square was a favorite place of ours, although it was usually full of old ladies who disapproved of boys like us. We had to watch our step, not scare away the pigeons they were feeding; and we couldn't smoke a cigarette, or they'd have scolded us.

Still, we came here almost every day. It was a mid-point, a kind of compromise between the very different worlds Armin and I came from. If you looked to the right, you could see the Klopstockstrasse and its fancy town houses; and, to the left, the Elbberg, where the scruffiest part of town began.

We kept meeting at the Balkon, even after I'd learned that I was half Jewish. Our friendship went on, didn't change. Because I didn't tell him. I didn't tell anyone. I wasn't allowed to. My father had forbidden it.

The morning after I found out, we had a "family council" at which it was decided (by my father, naturally) that, aside from ourselves and a few very close friends, my mother's origin was no one's business. According to her birth certificate, she was German, that was all. If word about her parentage got out, it would damage my father's law practice and make difficulties all around.

Yes, but I worried about the "few very close friends." I knew from overhearing conversations when my parents entertained how casual their friends could be about other friends' secrets. Someone talked, and soon everybody knew. I had to reckon with the probability that our secret would get out. Maybe it already had and had reached the Christianeum, where Dr. Knoppe (known to us as "the Ape") kept a list of non-Aryan students. Was my name already on that list?

The Ape was professor of Latin and Greek. He'd joined the faculty around the time when Hitler came to power. His legs were too short; his torso, too long and somehow crooked. He had a squashed-in nose and black hair, thin on top, but it sprouted thickly from his gaping nostrils. In other words, he did not look exactly the picture of a model Aryan. Nonetheless, he was a so-called old warrior, meaning he'd joined the Nazi party before 1927, when it was illegal and dangerous to belong.

One day while we were having our biology lesson with Schnurrbacher, who was not a Nazi sympathizer, the Ape appeared in our classroom with his list. *"Heil Hitler,"* he said, so abruptly that it sounded like *Heitler,* one word.

He and Schnurrbacher held a short, whispered discussion. We couldn't hear what was said. But I saw Schnurrbacher stiffen, purse his lips. And suddenly I grew very nervous.

72

Planting himself in the place of command, in front of the teacher's desk, the Ape consulted the list and began: "The Jews Cohn, Schneider, and Martini will step forward."

This was no surprise. We'd known right along about Cohn, and recently found out about Schneider and Martini too, although they didn't belong to a temple and were not religious.

The three got up. They slouched to the front of the room and stood beside the blackboard. An iron silence gripped the class. The Ape consulted the list again. I was sure he would read out my name next. But he just looked those three up and down, giving them the once-over, then made three check marks on the list, strode to the door, shot out his arm, barked another greeting— "Heitler!"—and was gone.

Cohn, Schneider, and Martini waited beside the blackboard. No one said anything. Schnurrbacher gazed out the window. Finally he turned around and told them, "You may go and sit down."

Heads bowed, they took their seats.

I didn't pity them. I had only one thought: *He didn't call* me! That meant they didn't know, because that list had half-Jews, even quarter-Jews, everyone with Jewish ancestors, on it.

The school knew only what appeared on my birth certificate: *German. Religion: Protestant.* Good.

But I wanted to tell Armin the truth. I had an obligation to. He was my best friend, my blood brother. We had sworn we wouldn't keep secrets from each other. Besides, since I was only a half-Jew, I figured he'd think the news was only half bad.

I'd started to tell him a few times, but I lost my nerve. I thought, *I'll wait for just the right moment to broach the subject,* and I put it off.

Then came April 1, 1933.

For weeks there'd been articles in the papers about how Jews in foreign lands were spreading anti-German propaganda, rumors, horror stories, shameless accusations, lies, all vicious lies! As a consequence, the Fatherland now faced a worldwide economic boycott.

GERMANY, DEFEND YOURSELF! the newspaper headlines blared, calling upon the nation to boycott Jewish businesses and stores, and Jewish doctors and lawyers, too. This boycott, the paper urged, should begin at once.

Posters were plastered on walls and kiosks: GERMANS, DO NOT BUY FROM JEWS! WORLD JEWRY IS OUT TO DESTROY US!

JEW was scrawled on store windows. SA men, HJ boys, and girls from the League of German Maidens stood guarding entrances, discouraging shoppers, taking photos of those who ignored them. In the meantime, some stores were broken into and looted.

On that day Armin and I were walking down the Königstrasse. Armin hadn't joined the HJ, because his father forbade it as strictly as mine.

We didn't talk as much about joining as we'd used to. I was still for the Nazis, but it was different now. Before, when they were the underdogs, they'd seemed like heroes. Now that they were in power, they didn't seem so daring anymore. They were the government. That made them less appealing.

The Königstrasse was going wild, people shouting, "Don't buy Jewish!" and so on.

"Look at that!" said Armin, laughing. He grabbed my shirtsleeve and pointed.

A man was running in the gutter. He was wedged between two signs, front and back, like the sandwich men who advertised department stores. He looked familiar, around forty years old, getting bald, with metal-framed glasses. Yes, I knew him: He owned a shoe store where my mother sometimes shopped.

He was exactly the kind of Jew I didn't like: He

spoke with a certain accent, fawned before customers, rubbed his hands a lot, and recommended only the most expensive shoes.

In the store he'd always smiled. Now he looked very serious, in his formal white shirt, stiff collar, necktie—and no trousers, just long underwear. I WILL <u>NEVER</u> MAKE ANOTHER COMPLAINT TO THE POLICE was written on the sandwich signs in ugly, wobbly lettering, with the word *never* thickly underlined.

Two *Schupos* followed a few meters behind him, making him run up and down that shopping street. We saw him again, twice, and both times Armin laughed about those signs as though he'd just heard a really good joke.

That day I decided not to tell him the truth about me. My name wasn't on the list the Ape took around from class to class. My father was an Aryan, a well-known attorney. He had served as an officer in the World War, had fought on the western front, and been awarded the Iron Cross. I was a German, period. I decided there was nothing to tell.

That night I lay awake a long time, thinking. I realized I would never join the HJ. Before, I'd told myself I'd do it, against my parents' will, told myself they couldn't stop me. That dream was over. The HJ investigated the racial origins of everybody who applied. I could not take that risk.

Oh, but I still wanted to be normal, to belong. I so wished to wear the snappy uniform, with the sheath knife tucked into my belt. Like Peter Mehlhorn, our class spokesman—he came to school dressed like that and went to HJ exercises every Saturday.

To march in step, in rows, in tight formation—I thought, *How splendid that must be.* The fellowship enlarged you, made you a better person, strong, undaunted, gave you purpose, and made everything clear.

Members of the HJ resolutely obeyed their squadron leaders. The squadron leaders obeyed *their* leaders, and so on, right on up. The highest-ranking leaders obeyed the Reich youth leader. And the Reich youth leader obeyed the Führer. In this way everyone obeyed the Führer, everyone belonged to one great body, and its name was Germany. No one had, or needed, a will or wishes of his own. Because the will of Germany was alive and throbbing inside everyone. And everyone was joined together into one great *Volksgemeinschaft*, a people's true community. . . . How I longed to be a part of it!

That was one reason why I clung ever closer to Armin, who, though not an HJ member, was a pure German. I went to his house as often as I could. His father didn't mind—he'd gotten used to me. When I was at the Hillmanns', it was easier to make believe I was like everybody else. I could forget I was half Jewish.

Life had improved a bit for them. Armin's father was still out of work, but the family now received allotments of coal for heating, potatoes, vegetables, and clothing from Winter Aid.

His mother was a plumpish woman, warm and friendly, who smiled a lot, although she always looked a little worried, which made her even more likeable.

Times were still hard, of course, and they were still short of everything. Often they had only watery soup or potatoes or cabbage for their midday meal or supper. But they always invited me to eat with them, and if one piece of meat was left in the pot, it always landed on my plate, no matter how much I protested.

When Armin came to my house, he almost never ate with us. If my father was home, it was out of the question. If my mother had a migraine, it was out of the question again—as though Armin being there could make the migraine worse!

Our house in the Flottbeker Chaussee was bright and spacious, and I had my own nicely furnished room. At Armin's everything was cramped. He slept in a sort of broom closet with nothing in it but his bed. The windows didn't close right, the wind blew in, and the walls were spotted with black mold. But I felt much more comfortable there.

The courtyard in the back was dark and reeked of cabbage. But in front, out on the street, children sat on the stoops and men stood around arguing, smoking. On our street no one ever stood around except servant girls, and you weren't supposed to stop and talk with them.

At our house everything went strictly according to schedule. Maria woke me up at seven sharp, Sundays and holidays, too. At twenty past seven I had to appear downstairs and wish my parents good morning. Then I ate breakfast, not in the dining room, but below stairs, outside the kitchen.

At Armin's everyone did what they liked, more or less. His mother was always busy doing housework. His father was usually out, and when he was home, he mostly slept on the sofa in the hall. Armin could come and go as he pleased.

At my house I had to demonstrate punctually at

eight o'clock that I had brushed my teeth, washed hands and face, and then go directly to bed. After much badgering, I'd finally received permission to read till nine.

Evenings at Armin's, his father often got home late from the bar. Then there'd be a big fight that ended with his mother snatching what money he had left and hiding it in various places where no one would think to look.

If her husband was still not home by midnight, Frau Hillmann sent Armin to get him. Sometimes I'd go along. Then it could happen that his father bought us a beer. If my parents had known, they'd have had fits. Unsuitable company! Uncouth lout! Well, they didn't know. And I would not give up being friends with Armin, no, never!

For the rest of that school year and the next, not too much changed for me. I stayed friends with Armin. Cohn, Schneider, and Martini left—voluntarily, it was said, to transfer to a Jewish *Gymnasium*. I stayed on, a student like any other, at least on the outside. One thing *did* happen: Armin joined the HJ, secretly, despite his father forbidding it.

RACIAL STUDIES

"LET ME INTRODUCE OUR NEW SUBJECT BY impressing on you that this area of knowledge is of utmost importance," Dr. Knoppe announced. He had been promoted to headmaster. While he talked, he entered the day's lesson plan into the class book as was customary, then closed the book, raised his head, and looked around benignly.

"And why is this subject, the science of race, of such importance?" he asked, starting to pace up and down. "Allow me to quote from our Führer, as he wrote in *Mein Kampf*: 'A nation which, in the era of racial poisoning, commits itself to nurturing its best and highest racial elements must, one day, become the master of the world.'"

Contorting his face into an exalted smile, he paused to let those words sink in.

"Race consciousness," the Ape continued, "awareness of distinct physical features must, as our Führer says, be burnished into your hearts and brains." He stopped pacing, leaned against the teacher's desk, and looked every student up and down. "You may already be familiar with certain concepts: purification; its opposite—namely degeneration; and, of course, the Nordic race. But let us proceed in proper order. Do you remember the Mendelian laws that you studied extensively last semester? Glucker?"

Martin stood up.

The Ape said, "Be so kind as to tell us what you recall."

Martin Glucker hemmed and hawed.

"Sit down!" barked the Ape, and called, "Hillmann!"

Armin jerked to his feet.

The Ape inquired, "Does the worthy gentleman remember the Mendelian laws?"

"Y-Yes," Armin stuttered.

"Good, I'm glad! And would you care to favor us with something more specific?"

"Well, if you cross a red rose with a white one, then, I think, a red, a white, and two pink roses will result."

"That is what you think?"

"Yes."

"Aha. And what is the name of this Mendelian law?"

"Um . . ."

Armin looked across the table to where Daniel sat. Daniel wanted to whisper to him, but the Ape stood too near.

Dr. Knoppe let Armin sweat for a few moments, then glanced around the class. "Can someone give our friend a hint? Kraushaar?"

Daniel stood up. "It's the second Mendelian law, the law of splitting."

"And what does it state?"

"That the third generation splits according to certain number ratios—that is, either three to one or one to two to one."

"And can you also refresh our memory regarding the inheritance of recessive traits?"

"When two races mix, the lesser race is dominant in the offspring. The higher race is recessive. That is, it gets weakened and destroyed by the lesser race."

"Very good. Sit down."

The Ape started pacing again. "Who can name the various human races? Mehlhorn?"

Peter Mehlhorn stood up. "First, there are the Germanic races: the Nordic, the Dinaric, the Falic . . ."

"And what can you say about the traits of these races?"

"These races are interrelated," Peter went on. "The noblest, highest is the Nordic. Its traits are mental superiority and a heroic, warrior nature. Nordic man is born to lead and therefore constitutes the master race."

"Thank you. Sit down. Can anyone tell us the proportion, roughly, of Nordic blood to other blood in Germany?"

Daniel raised his hand.

"Please."

"Roughly fifty percent."

"Correct. What other Germanic races do you know of?"

"The Dinaric, they are Alpine. This race also has excellent traits. For instance, the Führer is Nordic-Dinaric. Then, there are the Falic, the Ostic, and the Ost-Baltic. Those also have good traits, but members of those races are born to serve, not lead."

"And the other European races? Mehlhorn?"

Peter stood again. "The French, but they cohabited with Negroes and corrupted their blood, so now they almost can't be counted among European races anymore. The Slavs—they mixed with Asiatics, especially with Mongol hordes long ago. That made them unclean, untrustworthy, and incapable of cultural creation. Therefore, they are subordinate and must be kept under control."

"Very good. Hillmann, can you name other lesser races?"

Armin stood. "Yes, for instance, the Negroes."

"And what are their traits?"

"They are lazy and stupid."

"And is there an even lower race than Negroes?" asked Dr. Knoppe, feigning great curiosity.

"I don't think so," Armin said.

"Well, think a little harder."

Armin thought harder. "I don't know. Didn't you once say that the black race is the lowest human race?"

"Well, yes, I might have. In one sense it is true, because, speaking precisely, the very lowest race cannot be called human. I mean, of course, the Jewish race, also known as Semitic. It is the antirace. And why?"

Peter raised his hand.

"Please."

He stood. "The Jews are parasites. They feed off their hosts and produce nothing on their own. They are the dregs. There's nothing lower."

"Very good. Well now, we have learned from the science of inherited traits that when races are mixed, negative traits are dominant. So, when a Nordic person mates with someone of a lesser race—for instance, a Negro—then the Nordic person's good traits are lost. That is what our Führer means by racial poisoning, and that is precisely what the concept of degeneration means. Upstanding, cultivated races get destroyed by low ones." Dr. Knoppe raised his eyes and voice. "The dishonorable, dirty Jew looks with envy on the noble Nordic-German people. And inside every Jew there dwells a diabolic need to drag the noble race down into the muck with him. No reasonable farmer would ever allow such interbreeding of cattle! But among humans, to our shame, it happens every day."

The Ape made a fist. Then he pointed his index finger at an imaginary member of that loathed sub-human race. "The Jew has long been trying to besmirch and dishonor the Germanic race. Well, he hasn't succeeded! Fundamentally, our race is still healthy and clean. But our essential purity is under constant, daily threat. That is why it's so important to protect and, wherever possible, to strengthen the German people's racial traits. That task is of utmost urgency. We, each and all, must dedicate ourselves to it with vigilance and fervor."

The Ape wrinkled his brow and paused again for emphasis.

"It's well known," he went on, "that the Jew hankers obscenely after German women and that many German girls have fallen prey to his lust. This is the reason why there are so many mongrels, half-Jews and quarter-Jews, in Germany. As we have seen, half-Jews cannot be Nordicized because their Jewish blood component is too high. With quarter-Jews, it is different. They have only one Jewish grandparent and therefore *can* be rendered Nordic by marrying pure Aryans, which is the reason our government has made it mandatory that they do so, to prevent their Nordic blood from being lost."

The Ape took out his pocket watch, snapped it open. "We shall consider this material further during the next weeks. Then we shall have a look at the

personal family trees I've asked you for, as well as
undertake measurements of your skulls to see what
racial traits are represented in this third-year class.

"And now, I believe, we are finished for today.
Heil Hitler!"

The students stood up, stretched their right arms
forward, and shouted: *"Heil Hitler!"*

VOLGA GERMAN

ARMIN AND PETER WERE ALREADY OUT THE door. Daniel was still buckling his schoolbag. And then the Ape kept him from catching up with them.

"Ah, Daniel. Would you mind staying a moment?" His voice was oddly soft. And he almost never called students by their first names.

Daniel approached. The Ape stood at the teacher's desk, leafing through a folder—the one with the family trees. "The other students have handed theirs in," he said. "Yours is the only one missing."

He looked Daniel over, but in a friendly way. "You're usually well organized. Why haven't you given it to me?"

"Er, well, I didn't get everything together yet."

The Ape wrinkled his brow. "Is there a problem?"

Daniel had known that sooner or later the Ape would confront him. And he'd already thought of something. He'd gotten the idea from a boy in the parallel class, who'd said that his family was Volga German, repatriated only recently, so it was hard to trace his ancestry.

Fine, my mother can be Volga German, Daniel had decided, although her family had lived in southern Germany for generations. Daniel worried that this fact might get discovered, which is why he hesitated now.

"Is there a problem?" the Ape asked again.

"My mother, she . . ."

"She what?"

The classroom had emptied; they were alone. *This teacher likes me,* Daniel thought, and considered telling the truth.

"Out with it," the Ape said.

"My mother is a Volga German. She comes from Stalingrad." A rush of heat pulsed through him as he thought how far-fetched that must have sounded. "I mean, her parents came from there."

"Ah, yes, the Volga Germans," the Ape said pleasantly, "an admirable Aryan tribe. They have retained their true Germanic essence despite centuries of living among Russians and Tartars."

"Her parents didn't bring all their documents along when they were repatriated," Daniel explained, "so it's hard to trace her ancestry. . . ."

"Then just write 'Volga German.' That will do," the Ape said. "And hand it in next time, so we can get started measuring skulls, all right?"

THREE CLASS ASSIGNMENTS

Date: May 12, 1935
    Subject: Racial studies
    Teacher: Dr. Knoppe
    Theme: What experience have you or your family had with members of the Jewish race? Describe an occurrence in the form of an essay.

Peter Mehlhorn
My grandfather had a store. It was the time of the inflation. The Jews made the inflation happen in order to plunder us Germans.

At that time the Germans lost their hard-earned savings. My grandfather did too. And besides, buying things for his store got more and more expensive. It was the Jewish wholesalers' fault. My grandfather didn't want to be like them and raise his retail prices. He was an honorable man, and said, "I want to keep my good name." My mother told me that.

But his honesty didn't help. The store was losing money. He had to borrow from the bank. Soon the bank wouldn't lend him any more.

So Grandfather had to close down his store and rent it out. It became a shoe store. A Herr Katzenstein rented it. Nobody knew him, because he came from abroad, but my grandfather was glad he'd found a tenant. Even though he must have known what kind of tenant it was, just from the name Katzenstein. Because Katzenstein was a Jew.

My grandfather was a sick man, and that Jew, he buried him. That's what my mother says.

It started with Herr Katzenstein not wanting to pay so much rent anymore. He complained that business was bad, he said he sold too few shoes and the costs of everything were too high, especially the rent. My grandfather let him bargain it down. But soon after that, Katzenstein wrote my grandfather a letter—he should excuse it, but he couldn't pay any rent at all.

At first my grandfather believed the story. He knew himself how hard it was to keep a business going at that time. But then he saw that lots of people were still going into the shoe store and coming out with boxes of shoes. My grandparents lived in the same house, right over the store. So the Jew was making money, and not just a little. He just didn't want to pay rent, that was all.

So my grandfather went to a lawyer. That cost a lot of money too. But he wanted to bring the matter to court, so that Katzenstein would have to pay. All the shoes in the store, they were worth a lot.

Then suddenly Katzenstein came to see my grandfather. He pretended it was a misunderstanding and that they were the best of friends. And he kept saying, please don't go to court, he'd bring part of the money tomorrow, and the rest soon.

And he stood in front of the window so my grandparents couldn't see out. And he kept looking at his watch. My grandfather thought that was peculiar. But he didn't think anything bad about it. Katzenstein talked so much, my grandfather didn't hear it when a truck stopped in front of the house. Then Katzenstein looked out the window a few times, so my grandfather got the idea of looking out too. And he saw workmen dragging crates out of the store, loading them into the truck. They dragged out all the shoes. So then my grandfather understood what Katzenstein was up to, and right away he ran downstairs. But all he could do was watch the workmen load the last crate on the truck and drive away. He ran back upstairs to have serious words with Katzenstein, but meantime, he had vanished. As though the floor had swallowed him. No one ever heard of him again.

Grandfather never saw a penny of his rent. And Katzenstein undoubtedly has another shoe store someplace and is making lots of money.

My grandfather died soon after that. The Jew

brought him to his grave. That's what my mother always says.

Grade: Satisfactory.

You describe it vividly. But the cowardly, deceitful character of the Jews should have become a little clearer.

Grammar and sentence construction still leave much to be desired!

Dr. Knoppe

Armin Hillmann

In our house lives a Jew, his name is Silberstein, and he sells animal feed. He always goes on the ferry to the Old Land where the farms and orchards are. And here is a story I heard about him:

One time the ferry was very full and Silberstein sat next to a young girl. During the crossing Silberstein was very quiet, but suddenly he had to give in to an urgent bodily need, and very noisily. In other words, as one says, he farted. Then he looked at the girl next to him and said, "Don't worry about it, Fräulein, that happens to me too sometimes." Whereupon the young woman got angry and stood up. And here is another story I heard about him:

Again Silberstein took the ferry, but this time it was pretty empty. Silberstein sat down on a bench, and across from him sat a young woman. He went and

*sat next to her. He had a coat on. After sitting there
quietly for a while he opened his coat. Under it he
wore a jacket and pants, but he'd stuck a cow's teat
into his buttoned fly so that it looked like he was an
exhibitionist and as though a certain body part was
dangling out of his pants.*

*First the young woman didn't notice, but then she
looked, and she jumped up screaming. Then the other
passengers all noticed. Silberstein pretended to be
surprised and annoyed, and got out his pocketknife,
which frightened the young woman even more. Then
Silberstein cut the cow's teat off and said: "It's
always the same bother with that thing. Enough! I'm
getting rid of it!"*

*The young woman fainted and had to be carried
off the ferry in Altona.*

GRADE: PASSING

TO BE SURE, YOUR EPISODES SHOW A PARTICULARLY
UNPLEASANT SIDE OF THE JEW. HOWEVER, YOU SHOULD
ASK YOURSELF IF THEY ARE SUITABLE FOR A SCHOOL
ESSAY. I THINK NOT.

EXPRESSION, CHOICE OF WORDS, AND GRAMMAR
LEAVE MUCH TO BE DESIRED!

DR. KNOPPE

*Daniel Kraushaar
In the World War my father was at the western*

*front. His closest comrade at the front was a fellow
student—they had studied law in Freiburg and had
enlisted together. They'd known each other a long
time and were inseparable friends. What my father
didn't know, even then, was that his friend was a Jew.
Not someone you would recognize as Jewish by how
he looked or because he didn't eat pork. This friend of
my father's had resigned from the Jewish Community,
was baptized, and had become a Christian. And there
was nothing about how he acted that would have
pointed to his being Jewish; he always behaved
decently, and he and my father experienced many battles and waiting time in the trenches together.*

*But since the war lasted longer and longer, and
since they often had hardly anything to eat, the friend
grew discontent and complained that this war was
senseless and that there was no further hope that
Germany could win it. So my father said to him: "If
you say such things again, in front of our younger
comrades-in-arms who perhaps might believe you,
then there'll be an end to our friendship."*

*So the friend stayed quiet, didn't say such things
anymore. And for a while everything was all right. But
then he started to get interested in politics. At that
time the Communists were spreading their propaganda to the soldiers at the front. That made my father
furious. But his friend was interested in the leaflets
and the books and read them and believed every word.*

Then in winter 1917, when the Bolsheviks came to power in Russia, my father's friend started in again making speeches against the war. Again my father said he should stop, but this time he didn't stop, and so they had many quarrels. Finally came autumn of 1918. That was the time the war went into its critical phase. Russia had already been defeated, but in the West the German offensive had again come to a halt. And then came the news that the sailors in Lübeck were trying to start a revolution. For my father and many fellow soldiers, that was the last straw, but his friend, who had become a Communist, started a "Soldiers' Council" together with other Communists. They declared that the war was over, took the officers prisoner, and wanted everyone to march back to Berlin to support the revolution.

My father and other honorable soldiers refused and said: "We must stay here and hold fast to our Kaiser and fight for the Fatherland!" But the Soldiers' Council took their guns away and imprisoned them. My father told his friend that the friendship would be over and done with if he, the friend, went along. But the friend said he had to do his duty as a revolutionary, which was more important than friendship, and he let my father be taken prisoner.

My father was baffled. He didn't understand how this friend could betray him like that. Later, when the war was long over, he heard from the former friend,

*who, meantime, was not a revolutionary anymore, but
had earned a lot of money as a journalist. He also
found out finally that the friend was Jewish and
worked for a Zionist organization. When my father
found this out, then at last he understood.*

GRADE: GOOD!

YOUR NARRATION SHOWS DISTINCTLY HOW JEWISH
TREACHERY HAS INFLUENCED GERMAN HISTORY.

I AM VERY PLEASED WITH YOUR PROGRESS IN STYLE
AND GRAMMAR.

DR. KNOPPE

AFTER THE GAME

"NOTHING TO THREE," JÜRGEN SAID WITH a grin. They trotted down the endlessly long Hohenzollernring toward the Flottbeker Chaussee. It was a hot, humid Sunday afternoon.

"Nothing to three," Armin echoed.

Jürgen wiped his hand over his pimply forehead. "And we can't even have a smoke," he muttered.

Along the Hohenzollernring there were no corner cafés to go into with stories about buying cigarettes for their fathers. And the restaurants on the Flottbeker Chaussee were too refined to enter in sweaty jerseys and short pants with soccer boots dangling down their backs.

Then Daniel caught sight of Luigi Bianco, the ice-cream man. In summer he pushed his brightly painted cart through Altona and charged five pennies for a vanilla cone.

Ice cream was better than nothing, Daniel thought.

Jürgen and Armin didn't think so. If they spent

their last pennies on it, they wouldn't have any money for cigarettes.

"But we can't get any cigarettes," Daniel said.

Too true.

When they were sitting on the steps of the Elbpark with their dripping cones and looking down at the river, Armin and Jürgen returned to their subject:

"Nothing to three!"

"Nothing to three!"

Sunlight blazed on the water.

"And against Teutonia, of all teams!" Armin shook his head.

"Actually. the game shouldn't even count," Jürgen complained. "They have at least two non-Aryan players."

Armin nodded. "The shitty Jews bribed the umpire."

"Teutonia has Jews?" Daniel asked. "Who?"

Jürgen grinned bitterly. "Gluck-Gluck, for one."

Martin Glucker was in Daniel's and Armin's class. He did have a dusky complexion. "Too dark to be one hundred percent Aryan" was the prevailing opinion.

"But his skull measurement showed that he's Ostic-Dinaric," Daniel said. "And he handed in his family tree. That proves—"

"Not really," Armin said, closing his eyes.

102

"Everyone's skull measurement matches what's shown in the family tree. So, either all the family trees are perfect, or . . ."

"He does get very quiet when someone asks questions," Jürgen said.

Daniel didn't like this topic one bit. And lately there'd been more and more such talk about who might be non-Aryan. What were they saying about *him* behind his back?

"But his father is a Nazi Party member," Daniel said.

"You'd be amazed who all is in the Party," Armin observed.

"Troop Leader Kolinski always says that lots of people lie and try to hide what they really are," Jürgen said. "In your school too. But don't worry, we'll find them."

Jürgen was older, sixteen, and doing an apprenticeship, learning cabinetry. He didn't think much of snobby *Gymnasium*s and made no secret of it.

"So long, fellas," he said. "I have to get home. We're having company today." He shoved the rest of his ice cream into his mouth and stood up.

Armin and Daniel stood up too.

Jürgen exchanged hearty handshakes with them and left.

Armin and Daniel sat back down.

"I don't think there are any hidden Jews in our

school," Daniel said. "Everyone handed in family trees."

"So what? I told you, family trees can be false," Armin said. "Besides, nobody examined them." He paused as though he wanted to say more. He took a breath and went on. "That story about your mother . . . somehow it doesn't wash."

Daniel almost choked on his ice cream. He swallowed. "What do you mean?" he asked as calmly as he could.

A few days earlier, while the Ape was measuring Daniel's skull, he had given a long lecture about the excellent racial attributes of the Volga Germans. When he was done measuring, he declared that Daniel, brown hair notwithstanding, was primarily Nordic, no surprise, what with his mother a Volga German.

Armin had looked skeptical. And now he said, "You once told me your mother comes from Munich."

"Yes, because her family first moved there, and then they came here."

"You told it differently before."

"I didn't want to make a big to-do about it, so I just said she came from Munich."

"Hmm." Armin rubbed the back of his head. "I understand. But others might not. Jürgen, for instance."

"What might he not understand?"

"There've been rumors—"

"What kind of rumors?"

Armin looked down at the river. Two little tug-boats were pulling a giant freighter to the harbor.

After a pause he said, "Come on, Daniel, just join the HJ, and that'll be the end of it."

"Man, you know how much I want to!" Daniel said. "But my father—"

"Who cares about your father?" Armin shook his head. "Whoever doesn't join the HJ nowadays is either chronically sick or a Communist or . . . Well, anyway, you'd better, because otherwise, it doesn't add up."

"How doesn't it add up?"

Armin looked down at the river again.

"Go on. Say how."

"Why are you asking me?" Armin said. "I have no idea."

"No idea?"

"Stop. I just wanted to give you a tip. Because you're my best friend. What you do about it is your business." He turned to Daniel, looked him in the eyes. "I know you're on the right side. But there are a couple of big talkers. . . . I just wanted to protect you from . . . problems."

Daniel stood up.

"Thank you very much. But maybe you should mind your own business."

"All right," Armin said, "I will."

They dropped the subject. After a time Daniel said, "So long."

"UNCLE" KARL

WHEN DANIEL REACHED HOME, HE HEARD his father talking very loudly in the living room—unusual, since his father set great store by self-control.

His parents were quarreling, Daniel thought. But then he heard his father's friend and colleague's voice. Daniel still called him "Uncle Karl," even though they really weren't related.

Karl was his father's best and just about only friend.

The people the Kraushaars saw socially were really close only to Sophie. Daniel thought his father must have had more friends when he was young but probably had alienated them with his rigid ways.

Rheinhard's only other friend was an old army crony who came once a month to play chess. But he usually arrived late, after Daniel had gone to bed. All Daniel knew about him was that he'd lost one leg and a hand in the war, that he smoked cheap cigarettes which smelled up the room, and that the morning after a visit his father would be in a bad mood, especially if he had lost at chess. Rheinhard spoke unkindly of him and made it clear that he let him visit merely because he felt sorry for him.

Daniel took his soccer clothes into the laundry room, then stopped quietly in the foyer. Rheinhard and Karl had obviously not heard him enter the house. Since Sophie was out and Maria had the afternoon off, the two men spoke as though they were alone.

Rheinhard sounded agitated. "If you have something to say, then say it."

Daniel could hear his father pacing up and down the room.

Karl answered soothingly, "You are a brilliant attorney, Rheinhard. Everyone knows that. And I'm aware that I owe you a great deal."

Daniel knew this conversation wasn't for his ears. But if he went up to his room now, the stairs would creak, and his father would know he'd been listening. So he stayed in the dim foyer, studying the golden pattern on the brocaded wallpaper as Karl talked on— about the situation in the law office, which had become untenable, and about a meeting at the Ministry of Justice to which he'd been invited.

"What did they say to you?" Rheinhard asked. "The usual allegations?"

"You are not the problem," Karl replied.

"Then who is?" Rheinhard's voice now sounded

calm, but Daniel knew: This was how his father sounded just before the storm.

There was a pause. Daniel imagined the scene. Probably, Rheinhard lit a cigarette, although he often said that smoking when one was excited was a bad idea.

"I don't enjoy this situation any more than you do," Karl said very softly.

Rheinhard didn't answer.

"Let me make a suggestion," Karl went on. "Wouldn't it be best for everyone if you—just as a formality, just for the time being . . ."

He didn't finish the sentence, but Daniel knew at once where this speech was heading. He wondered why he, Daniel, hadn't thought of it himself. It seemed so obvious. It would be absolutely no problem for an Aryan like Rheinhard to untangle himself from his Jewish wife and half-Jewish son. This sort of thing was happening more and more often.

But Rheinhard seemed not to have understood his friend.

"What do you mean?" he asked.

"I mean," Karl said reluctantly, "if you divorced—"

"My dear Karl," Rheinhard interrupted in a quiet, cutting voice, "do not dare to speak of this ever again in my presence."

"Rheinhard, I'm sorry that I . . . ," Karl said.

Daniel pictured him fiddling with his cigarette case.

"It's all right," Rheinhard said. "Have a seat, Karl."

"No, thank you. I prefer to remain standing."

Father must have known this day was coming, must have been expecting it, Daniel thought.

A few weeks earlier, when the provisions of the Nuremberg Laws were announced in the press, Rheinhard had spent horrid moments reading them in black on white, in high judicial German: Sexual intercourse between Jews and Germans was now regarded as racial ignominy, shame, and punishable as such. Mixed marriages were henceforth forbidden. Furthermore, German women under forty-five could no longer be employed by Jews as household workers. Did that new law apply to their maid, Maria?

Drastic as these interdictions were, they merely gave legal status to what had been in effect for some time. It was true that some mixed marriages—namely, those with offspring—were to be tolerated.

However, Rheinhard's case was exceptional.

He was a prominent attorney, moving in high-ranking political circles, as Karl had correctly observed. Jews and half-Jews so much in the public eye were being regularly forced to resign their positions, whether they'd been front-line fighters in the World War or not.

Clearly, Rheinhard was a thorn in the Nazis'

sides. World opinion forced them to leave some mixed marriages alone, but if one spouse was a prominent figure, then they were eager to erase the stain, if not legally, then by other means:

Nasty articles in the widely read daily *Völkischer Beobachter.* Even nastier ones in the rabid tabloid *Stürmer*. Photos of Aryan husbands who pigheadedly refused to divorce Jewish wives. Headlines blaring, RACE ABOMINATION! Cartoons of mongrel children, ugly little half-Jews with hook noses, still shamefully attending German schools.

And letters from outraged readers.

No such letters about us, Daniel thought, *at least that I know of.* . . . But he was pretty sure there'd been telephone calls. Anonymous. Insulting. To his father at the office. Not at home . . . as yet.

Now someone at the office must have dropped a hint. That was how slander campaigns started. Perhaps it was somewhat reassuring that Karl said he'd been "invited" to the Justice Ministry, indicating that the Kraushaar matter was to be handled more discreetly, merely with threats.

"Divorce," Rheinhard said. Daniel pictured his father, looking straight at Karl. "Would *you* abandon your wife and child?"

"It would just be temporarily," Karl said. "Sophie and Daniel could wait abroad till things get back to normal, as they surely will. Daniel could continue his schooling there. And you could earn enough money here to support them both."

"Just 'temporarily'?" Rheinhard questioned.

That word had been used again and again in the two years since Hitler had taken power. People said the Nazis couldn't last much longer. Rheinhard had used the word himself, many times, saying that it was just a matter of time till the "mischief" would be over.

There stood Karl—Daniel pictured him in his double-breasted suit, fiddling with his silver cigarette case—suggesting divorce!

Did Rheinhard now ask himself why he had furthered this man's career? Why he had tried to make a good attorney out of him?

At least Karl had the tact to let the subject drop. Probably, he now sat down on the sofa, lit his cigarette. They were quiet. Then Karl started speaking of his brother Johann. "You met him at my house once, do you remember?"

"The furniture manufacturer?" Rheinhard asked. "What does he have to do with this? Is Johann by chance also married to a Jewess?"

"Johann's company could use a leading jurist," Karl said. "You could have a secure position, less exposed to scrutiny. And you'd earn more than you do now."

"I'm not looking for a position," Rheinhard said.

"Haven't you grasped our situation yet?" Karl

asked. "The firm doesn't have any other choice!"

"What should I do at your brother's?" Rheinhard went on. "I don't know anything about business. And absolutely nothing about furniture. I am a defense attorney."

"You'll soon work your way into it," Karl said.

"I repeat, I'm not looking for work. I have a going practice."

"*We* have a practice," Karl said. "One not solely depending on you."

"No?"

"You can't direct it any longer."

"What are you saying?"

"You have to cede its leadership to me."

"At last the cat's out of the bag," said Rheinhard. Karl protested. "I'm not the one who wants this!"

"And if I don't agree?" Rheinhard asked.

"Then I don't know what more to say."

Daniel was stuck in the foyer all this time. Now, guessing from the dead end the conversation had reached that Karl would be leaving any moment, he took his boots off and dashed upstairs in his stocking feet.

FAMILY SCENE

AFTER RHEINHARD HAD SHOWN KARL TO the door, he stood on the veranda, watching his colleague cross the street and climb into his blue Cabriolet.

Karl looked back; their glances met. Then he started the motor.

What next? Rheinhard asked himself. *Must I step down, agree to being replaced? Accept being demoted by an assistant in my own law practice? And if not, will Karl allow the Jurists' League to cast me out? Or will he risk his own professional future for my sake? Why wouldn't he, since he's so sure that things will soon be back to normal?*

"I thought I saw Karl drive by," Sophie said, climbing the last two steps.

"You did. He was here."

"What for?"

"He brought some rather disconcerting news—"

"I have some too," she interrupted nervously. "I ran into Hannerl at the market, Ilse Kleinfeld's sister, remember? And she told me that the Kleinfelds have left. For Prague. Yesterday, all of a sudden. They hardly took anything with them. They didn't even say good-bye!"

"Really? I'm sorry to hear that. I know you'll miss them."

"I will. And I take it as a sign that *we* should . . ." She let the sentence dangle. "But tell me, what was Karl's news?"

They sat down in the living room. Rheinhard started, "Oh, he talked about the situation in the office. It's becoming . . ." He halted. "*You* know, problematic. . . ."

Sophie paled, clasped her hands, squeezing her fingers tightly together. "Not just 'problematic.' Worse. 'Untenable,' he must have said. Well, didn't he? And what does he want you to do about it?"

"I thought he was my friend," Rheinhard murmured.

"All right, don't tell me what he said. I can guess. Your 'friend' Karl wants you to divorce me. Isn't that right? Like Otto Müller divorced Elfriede. That way Otto stays director of his company, and it works out fine—for him. Well, why don't you? What are you waiting for?"

"Sophie, stop! You know perfectly well that it's out of the question."

"You want to stay married? You're sure? Then we

have to get away! Before it's too late!" Sophie said.

Rheinhard shook his head. "We've been over all that. And we agreed—"

"No, *you* agreed."

"I've told you and told you. I don't have enough background in international law. I wouldn't be able to qualify as a lawyer in any other country. Here I have a good income. We can wait it out. Hitler won't stay in power forever."

"Really? Why not?"

"I know it sounds like wishful thinking. I'm serious, though. Conditions are atrocious. Our country has sunk to its all-time low. But all-time lows have one advantage: Things can't get worse, they can only improve. It may take a few years. But we'll manage, you'll see. Luckily, we're not in immediate danger. And rather than emigrate into the blue—"

"You know that my cousin in Brussels would take us in," Sophie said.

"It would take years before I could earn money there. They don't exactly need German jurists in Belgium."

"I'd rather work as a cleaning woman in any other country than stay here while things get worse and worse," Sophie cried out, more and more frantic. "I don't want to wait till it's too late! If you insist on staying, do. But my son and I have to leave while we still can!"

Now she was screaming. Upstairs, Daniel heard and came rushing down. "Not me, I'm not leaving!" he declared.

"You've been eavesdropping?" Rheinhard accused him.

"Not my fault, she screamed so loud." And Daniel repeated, "I'm not leaving. I want to stay in Germany."

Sophie reached a hand toward him but kept standing where she was.

"All my friends are here," Daniel said. "I'm a German. Why should I leave? Because you are a Jewess?"

"Don't speak like that to your mother," Rheinhard growled, and turned sharply away.

"But it's the truth!" Daniel exclaimed. "Because she's a damned Jewess we can't stay here anymore?"

"We can very well stay here." Rheinhard turned back to Daniel and gave him a piercing look. "You will never speak to your mother in this tone again."

She moved toward Daniel, saying, "Yes, I'm 'a damned Jewess,' at least by the Nazis' definition, and you're a half-Jew, whether it suits you or not. And no one can know how things in Germany will develop. And that is why I will take you somewhere else."

"You go," Daniel said. "But don't take me. I don't want to live abroad with some relative or other. I want to stay here. I'm a German."

"I'm a German too," Sophie said. "But the Germans don't want us. Not me and not you."

"You two going alone is *out of the question*! The family must stay together. And as long as it's not imperative to leave, we will stay in Germany. End of discussion," Rheinhard said. He went into his study and shut the door.

A TROUBLED NIGHT

THAT NIGHT, VERY LATE, A TAXI PULLED UP at the Kraushaars' house. Its noisy brakes woke Rheinhard. Sophie slept on, then jolted upright when the doorbell rang.

"Don't be alarmed. I'll go down," Rheinhard said, groping for his housecoat in the dark.

Sophie switched the light on and put on her robe. They both went downstairs.

At the door stood a young woman with a suitcase in her hand. Seeing them look alarmed, she burst into tears.

"Miriam!" Sophie pulled her inside and embraced her.

"I woke you up, I'm sorry—"

"It's all right, don't cry." Sophie smoothed her niece's shiny black hair. "You must be exhausted. Come." She took Miriam by the hand, led her upstairs to the guest room, and almost wordlessly helped her into bed.

"Why didn't Sebastian notify us that she was coming?" Rheinhard asked once Sophie joined him in their bedroom.

"I couldn't ask her anything. She was so tired, she fell asleep with one kneesock still on. Something must have happened. Listen, Rheinhard, she's my—"

"I know, I know, your only brother's only child. She'll tell us in the morning. Meantime, come to bed. We need our rest."

"It's something terrible, I just know it. They must have come for Sebastian—"

"Hush. It's pointless to assume the worst. Let's go to sleep."

"I can't sleep, I'm too worried! Rheinhard, talk to me!"

"Very well, if you'll calm down. Whatever the reason Miriam came, you have to realize that if she stays, we cannot keep the truth a secret. She's Jewish by birth and upbringing. She'd have to go to a Jewish school—"

"Where she'll at least learn something sensible," Sophie broke in, "something other than racial hygiene and German remilitarization."

"That may be. But her presence would make it obvious that you are Jewish," Rheinhard continued, "and that ours is a mixed marriage."

"Fine," Sophie said. "I'm tired of playing hide-and-seek. And, anyway, everyone I care about already knows."

"A few friends know. My clients don't. The judges don't. Daniel's teachers don't."

"Then get a divorce! What are you waiting for?"

"I beg you, don't start with that again!" Rheinhard turned to the wall, closed his eyes.

Sophie stared into the dark and spoke in broken whispers. "She's only fifteen years old . . . she came here all alone . . . if it's what I'm so frightened of, Sebastian's in prison or someplace worse." She sobbed. "Rheinhard, don't make me send her home!"

"What do you take me for?" He turned to her and pulled her close. "Miriam will stay, of course. For as long as necessary."

They slept at last, Rheinhard soundly, Sophie restlessly. Sometime later a faint rustling sound awoke her. Something light—an envelope—came sliding in under the door.

Sophie got out of bed, picked it up, and went to her dressing alcove. There she read the letter it contained.

THE LETTER

DEAR SOPHIE,

It's not easy, having to appeal to your sisterly feelings for me.

By the time you read this, bad will have come to worse. The thing I almost haven't dared imagine, that robs me of sleep, will have happened.

I'm giving this letter to a friend to keep and hope I'll soon be able to retrieve it myself. But if it finds its way to you, then the men in gray will have visited me, those who don't take off their hats when they enter an apartment and who don't ever give their names—then I will have been "called for," meaning taken away.

This danger has been hanging over me for months. I have done nothing the state defines as wrong, but apparently my mere existence is seen as a transgression. You know where I stand politically and what I've said and written. How can I deny it?

Maybe, if I close down this store from which, in any case, I can sell only the most innocuous books, *they'll leave me in peace. But then, what would Miriam and I live on?*

I tried to find a way to make it possible for Miriam to go abroad. But no one is prepared nowadays to take in a Jewish girl from Germany unless she brings along a lot of money: not the English, not the French. Not Holland, not Switzerland; as you know, they haven't let in any Jewish refugees in a long time. Going to Palestine becomes increasingly difficult, and besides, to send the child in the truest sense into the desert, into hostile surroundings . . .

For me to emigrate at this time is totally impossible. It seems I missed my one and only chance of getting out of Germany early in '33, when Max went to Palestine. He was going to open a store there and wanted me for his partner.

Why didn't I go? It's tragic but also comical; I almost have to smile, thinking of the frantic, futile efforts I've been making these past months—and back then I could have gone without any problems! I could have sold the bookstore and taken the money along. But no, because I told myself that Germany, my Fatherland, needed me more than ever.

But let me not bore you with all that has happened in these last years.

I know I should have gotten in touch. And I thank you for all your attempts to maintain closer contact. As it happens, I did telephone one time but lost my courage and hung up. I had too many other worries, and also I was too proud. . . .

As I said, if this letter reaches you, bad will have come to worse. I must expect it first thing tomorrow morning. Miriam is spending the night at a class-mate's. She knows how things stand with me but does not know about the acute danger—I didn't want to alarm her unnecessarily.

She's a wonderful girl, and I know you'll be good friends.

They made her change schools. That was very painful for her. Now she's passionately Zionist and wants to go to Palestine. You know how I feel about that. But all right, if it gets her out of this country . . .

The friend to whom I entrust this letter will bring her to the train to Hamburg and give her money for a ticket. When the thing I dread is behind us, you will hear from me.

In the hope that this letter will never have to be delivered, I remain your loving brother,

Sebastian

NEXT MORNING

DANIEL HAD ALREADY LEFT FOR SCHOOL when his parents came down to the breakfast room, Rheinhard anxiously tapping the folded letter against his left palm.

Sophie called Maria and asked her to set another place at the table.

Soon Miriam came down, looking pale but composed, neatly dressed, hair freshly brushed. "Good morning," she said faintly.

Maria brought her a hazelnut-filled crescent and slices of buttered raisin bread. Sophie poured her a cup of *Milchkaffee*.

"Someone's here," Rheinhard said. "I heard the front door open." In a moment Daniel appeared at the stairs leading down to the breakfast room.

"What are you doing back from school so early?" Rheinhard asked.

"Special exercises," Daniel said, staring at Miriam. "What's *she* doing here?"

"Daniel! Is that how you greet your cousin?"

Sophie scolded, sounding pained.

"*Hallo*, Daniel," Miriam said shyly.

"*Hallo*," he muttered almost inaudibly, and turned toward the hall.

"Stop," Rheinhard called. "What 'special exercises'?"

"HJ, the ones I'm banned from," Daniel answered, taking three steps at a time.

Later that morning—Rheinhard had left for work, Miriam was unpacking in the guest room—Sophie knocked at Daniel's bedroom door.

He didn't invited her to come in.

She entered anyway. He lay reading.

"I want to talk with you about Miriam," she said, sitting on the bed beside him.

Daniel did not look up. As far as he was concerned, there was nothing to discuss.

He'd peeked into the guest room, seen the suitcase—she was moving in! Naturally, nobody had asked his opinion. And why, of all names, did hers have to be Miriam? No German girls were called that.

Now everything would soon be all too clear. Everyone would know that a Jewess lived with them. And that she was Daniel's cousin. And that Daniel's mother was a Jewess. And that he was a half-Jew.

It made emigrating seem suddenly not such a bad idea. *Yes, emigrate, just vanish, see no one here ever again. Then no one would find out.*

But he didn't feel like talking about that with his mother.

She explained what a hard time Miriam had been through and went on about some sort of serious trouble Uncle Sebastian was in. She spoke to Daniel as though he were a child. Didn't she realize he could figure out on his own that Sebastian most likely had gotten himself put in jail or into a concentration camp?

"You could try to cheer her up a little," Sophie said. "Maybe go for a walk with her." As though that would be the most normal thing in the world. She smiled at him and asked, "Aren't you just a little glad to have such pleasant female company?"

She's treating me not like a child—no, like an idiot, Daniel thought. Going for a walk. In the park. Where, at any moment, he could run into someone. Then how would he introduce her? *This is my cousin, Miriam. Her hooked nose looks pretty, don't you think? And by the way, I'm a* Mischling. Mischling *first degree. Half-Jew. So long, good day!*

His mother knew about all that; she had to! So how could she sound as though there were no problems, none at all?

Daniel didn't answer her.

She went to the door and stood there waiting, hoping he'd say something. Then she sighed in great sorrow and left.

A LETTER NOT WRITTEN

DANIEL WENT TO HIS DESK, PICKED UP SOME writing paper and his fountain pen, and sat on the edge of his bed. He wanted to write a letter to Armin. He had to let him know. Sooner or later his friend would find out, so the truth had better come from Daniel.

He stared down at the lined paper. What should he write? He couldn't start with *Dear Armin*—that would sound like a love letter. Whenever he'd written him postcards from vacations, he'd always put *Hallo, Armin,* or just *Heh!*

But those weren't right for this letter.

He drew zigzag lines across the page. After a while he balled the paper up and threw it in the wastebasket.

He sat and thought. Something about their friendship was changing. It had nothing to do with Armin belonging to the HJ. More to do with growing up, reaching—what was it called? Adolescence? Puberty? Something like that.

Armin was reaching it. Daniel, not yet.

One difference was that a topic they'd hardly bothered mentioning before—girls—Armin now found very interesting. Lately, when they were going someplace, he would suddenly stop and stare after some girl as though spellbound, especially if she was "well developed," as he said.

If they were sitting together with Jürgen, Erwin, and others from the soccer team, there'd be endless talk about certain girls—their legs, their figures, and especially their breasts, or rather, "titties," "milk jugs," "melons," "boobs," and so on. Or they'd put their own lyrics to hit songs and burst out laughing at the juicy parts—for instance, getting one's fingers bloody groping some girl's underwear. Daniel would laugh along with the others, but he didn't understand. What was so funny?

One time Armin, after wolfing down his sandwich, had recited: "'After eating, try a smoke / Or a woman you can poke / If you can't, that's all right too / The good old hand machine will do.'" The others knew instantly what it meant. But Daniel didn't and thought, *I'm obviously retarded*. Once when his class was at the swimming pool, fat Erwin came up behind him, held him fast with one hand, and with the other reached into Daniel's bathing trunks, touched everything, and then cried, astonished, "Really, no hair yet!"

Of course he knew one was supposed to have pubic hair at his age.

But Armin didn't care. It made no difference to him that Daniel was backward in these matters.

They stayed best friends. And now that Miriam was moving in with the Kraushaars for who knew how long, Daniel felt he had to confide in Armin.

He'd feel relieved when someone knew, and he wouldn't always have to keep it secret anymore. So he began to write:

To Armin.

Next, an awkward sentence announcing that he had something urgent to confide.

Daniel put the pen down.

And then he imagined the Ape smack in front of him, and, yes, he knew exactly what the Ape would do once the secret was out:

Aha, a half-Jew! He'd retake Daniel's measurements promptly. In front of the whole class. And this time he would reach a different conclusion. *Note the angle of the nose, the telltale curvature at the base of the skull* . . .

Actually, Daniel wanted to go on with the letter, but he couldn't see the paper on his lap, only the classroom on the second floor of the Christianeum.

The scene played like a film before his eyes: He sat across from the teacher's desk as everyone stared. And the Ape asked, *Which identifying traits of the Jewish race do you discern in this face?*

Armin looked away. The others raised their hands

and answered: The lips. Too thick for a true Aryan. The hair, too curly. That means there's Negro blood mixed in. It's a well-known fact that the Jewish race comprises many such inferior elements.

And the Ape nodded approvingly every time.

Finally the Ape asked, *What else do you see in this face?* And when no one raised his hand, he gave the answer himself: *We see a cowardly, deceitful expression here. That is the most characteristic, essentially Jewish trait.*

Daniel thought, *It's true of me. I am a coward and deceitful.*

And suddenly he heard a voice inside himself saying, *You lied to them all. Even to Armin, your blood brother. Yes, you are a coward and deceitful. Just like a real, unmistakable Jew.*

Daniel hoped that writing the letter, admitting the truth, would silence the voice and set things right, at least with Armin. He took up the pen again.

He tried several times to get past that first awkward opening.

Each new try seemed stiffer, more pathetic than the last.

He pushed away the writing paper and leaned back.

He was not at all tired, yet he felt totally spent.

And then it came to him that Armin would never forgive him.

Or maybe Armin *would* forgive him, but he'd break off the friendship. Armin would have to. Daniel thought, *I would, if I were in his place. Who'd want to be friends with a half-Jew?*

He balled up the letter he'd begun. He decided he would never tell. No one must find out.

A LETTER NOT SENT

DEAR PAPS!

I would love to write to you. But I don't even know where you are. Sophie went twice to the police and asked. Uncle Rheinhard also tried to find out. He knows someone at the Ministry of Justice.

I have to confess something. I read your letter. The one to Sophie. On the train. I just had to know what you wrote. But I skipped the personal parts.

I can understand that you didn't want to tell me about the threat. But maybe it would really have been better.

Sophie is very nice. But of course I notice that I'm a problem for her. You have to imagine it: Daniel goes to a German Gymnasium *and keeps it a secret that he's half Jewish. Rheinhard and Sophie are secretive too. They don't go out; they see only close friends. How long can that go on?*

Naturally, I am a difficulty. But what should I do? I can't go home. Sophie thinks it doesn't matter, because the whole business of pretending will soon not work anymore.

So, Paps, you know anyway that I miss you. We can skip that.

I would like to send you something to eat or something warm to wear. The weather is starting to get cool. Mornings, when I go to school, the leaves are flying off the trees and forming big heaps behind the garden fences.

Daniel refuses to walk with me, even though we go the same way till the Altona town hall. The other day there was a pretty bad scene about that.

"I'm not walking with the Jewess," he said. I felt like running out of the room.

Daniel got a slap in the face from his father.

Do I look that Jewish? Probably. My nose . . .

It's awful. You get that propaganda stuffed into your ears so long, you start believing it yourself. Sometimes I think there must be something to it. Obviously, no one likes Jews. Even Jews don't. And then I think that somehow we must be worse than other people, and I start to feel that there's nothing we can be proud of.

Germany wants to throw us out—but no country lets us in. They all have enough already. If the Jews are such a first-rate people, then why doesn't anybody want us? Not even Madagascar will let us come and settle there.

It's interesting: On the street you know right away who's Jewish. I don't mean the Orthodox with their hats and curled sideburns. I mean the ones in normal clothes. I recognize them by how they walk. The Jews always stay close to the building walls. Or near the gutter. Even though it isn't written anywhere that they should. And they always look down. As though they are looking for something on the ground. And there's always this embarrassed smile. As if they wanted to beg pardon for something. No Germans walk in that crept-inside-themselves way.

I know what you always say: It's a mark of distinction to have this barbaric horde for enemies. And there is no reason to feel ashamed. But I can't manage it anymore.

Because sometimes I catch myself walking like that. Head lowered. And then I'm ashamed because I have such black hair. And I'm ashamed because I'm defenseless against the boys who lie in wait for us in front of the school and throw horse manure and stones at us. And I'm ashamed of the way the SA men look at us. And I'm ashamed of being ashamed.

But the way Daniel's friend, this Armin, looks at me . . . It doesn't bother him that I have black hair. On the contrary. His eyes practically pop out.

He was here the other day. They were going to soccer practice together. Daniel said if they didn't leave right away, they'd be late. But Armin kept find-

ing excuses to stay another moment. And he kept giving me these looks.

Or am I just imagining it? He's pretty handsome. Blond, blue-eyed, with a crooked smile . . .

It doesn't matter. There's no way anything could start between us.

Now I've written such a lot. And I don't even know where I could send this letter to you.

So I will keep it.

Your daughter,

Miriam

P.S. Sometimes, just before I fall asleep, when it's dark all around me, so dark that I can't see anything, I imagine that I'm home, in the Kettlerstrasse, and then I think I hear your footsteps in the kitchen, where you're making yourself a cup of tea. . . . And then I hear your voice; you're talking to someone on the telephone. . . . And then I think, "Tomorrow, when I get up, we'll sit together at the breakfast table."

AT SOCCER PRACTICE

WHEN ARMIN AND DANIEL ENTERED, THE changing room grew noticeably quiet. The only sound was Erwin's cleats on the floor as he strapped them to his boots.

Jürgen stopped talking in midsentence and stood there in his size-large undershorts merely looking at the two of them.

When the conversation resumed, it was about the usual subject: HJ duty—the past weeks' outdoor exercises and the weekly "Home Evenings" devoted to political instruction about the Führer's extraordinary achievements and the loathsomeness of the Jews.

"Very soon now all the Jews will get their asses ripped open," Jürgen declared loudly, looking straight at Daniel.

"Where's Coach?" Armin asked quickly.

"He's not coming today," said Klaus, the team captain.

Jürgen kept staring at Daniel. Daniel sat, started to lace up his soccer boots.

Did Jürgen know something? He'd been giving him those looks and dropping dark hints about racial origins for weeks. He'd started shortly after Miriam moved in. So far the others hadn't taken his remarks too seriously, or if they had, they didn't let on.

Daniel jogged outside and ran the track, both to cool down his anger and warm up for practice. Jürgen came after him, needling, "Do you really think it's such a good idea?"

Daniel gave him a blank look.

"I mean, your coming to soccer." Jürgen turned his head, directing Daniel's attention to the grandstand from which hung a big sign: JEWS AND DOGS NOT WANTED.

Daniel made no reply.

Jürgen wiggled his behind at him and trotted off.

Did he know? And if he knew, why didn't he just say it loud and clear?

Daniel tried to reassure himself: *Jürgen has never liked me, and it's mutual. He likes me even less now that I'm playing his position on the field.*

Daniel wouldn't have minded staying a substitute player if that would have kept Jürgen's trap shut. But he couldn't very well go up to the coach and ask to be put back on the bench. Besides, he felt proud that he'd finally gotten a first-team position.

That day, team captain Klaus took charge of the practice.

After everyone lined up in two facing groups, Daniel noticed that Jürgen, Egon, and their whole bunch were holding a whisper session.

He knew he had to be on his guard.

Klaus blew the whistle. The ball landed near Jürgen, who in fact was a pretty good player. His strength was dribbling, and it was his greatest weakness, too. He did it so well, he never wanted to pass. He dribbled himself into a tight knot of opponents somewhere on the sideline.

"Pass!" Klaus bellowed. "Pass the ball!"

Someone kicked it away from Jürgen. It landed near Armin. He shot it across to Daniel.

Daniel's great strength was speed. He maneuvered the ball halfway across the field. No one could follow him. Only Egon, the replacement forward, was still between him and the goal. Daniel slowed down, shifted the ball to his left foot, body faked, turned off to the right, and Egon sprinted past him. Feeling quite relaxed, Daniel scooted the ball over the goal line and let himself fall casually into the net.

Klaus gave another whistle and called out, "One to nothing!"

Returning to midfield with the ball under his arm, Daniel tried to sidestep Jürgen. Jürgen bumped into him as though accidentally.

When Daniel turned around, Jürgen tore the ball away. His features contorted, he hissed something incomprehensible—except for the word *Jew*—and, with all his weight, rammed into Daniel.

Daniel stumbled backward. Jürgen kicked out with one foot. Daniel managed, in the nick of time, to roll over on his side.

Jürgen's kick missed. He lost his balance and fell.

A circle gathered around them. Jürgen scrambled up, hurled himself on top of Daniel, and started to beat him with his fists.

Daniel held his arms up to protect his face. He heard Jürgen breathing hard, he felt his lip burst open, then a biting pain in the bone of his nose. Without forethought, he clutched Jürgen and pulled him tight against his chest to ward off further blows.

Then he saw Armin standing over them, pulling Jürgen off, and Klaus stepping between them. Klaus grabbed hold of Jürgen's right arm and of Armin's left.

"Let go of me!" Jürgen yelled. "I'll finish the Jew swine off!"

Armin and Klaus held him fast.

Daniel sat halfway up and saw that Jürgen, too, was bleeding from the nose.

Klaus shouted at Jürgen, "Quiet! Have you gone crazy? In the middle of practice?"

Jürgen freed his arm and wiped the blood from his face.

Armin helped Daniel to his feet.

"Helping the Jew swine?" Jürgen hissed.

"Shut up!" Klaus said, still holding on to him.

"I refuse to play on a team with a Jew bastard," Jürgen spat. "He should go to Palestine, where he belongs."

Armin turned toward Jürgen. "What did you say?"

"He should go to Jerusalem, the stinking Jew."

"Screw you," Armin said.

"I'm just speaking the truth," Jürgen answered.

"You're full of it," Armin said. "You're just pissed that he's got your position on the team."

Jürgen jerked himself free and grabbed Armin.

Klaus tried to separate them.

Then Egon mixed in. He pulled Jürgen to the side and muttered, "Let it alone. He really doesn't know yet."

Then he turned to Armin and said, "Your bosom buddy is a *Mischling*."

The others stood around nodding, agreeing. One said, "Exactly." Then a stillness set in.

Daniel saw the whole thing—he saw himself, too—as though from a distance, as though from the edge of the playing field, over by the grandstand. He saw how Armin confronted Jürgen.

"Stop that shit," Armin cried.

"Ask him yourself," Jürgen said.

"Yes, ask your friend," Egon echoed. "Ask if he's an Aryan."

Armin stood there with his arms hanging limp. Jürgen grinned, and some of the bystanders jeered.

Armin turned to Daniel. "Why are you letting this happen?"

"He should be thankful we put up with him this long," Jürgen said. "But now it's over."

"What's going on, Daniel?" Armin asked. "Why don't you say something?"

"Why *don't* you say something?" Egon repeated.

They all stared at him.

Daniel wanted to answer. But his brain felt numb. A stupid hit song circled in his head, like a record with a crack in it.

"Why don't you say anything?" Jürgen asked.

Suddenly the song stopped. Daniel saw everything around him as though he'd just arrived: the scraggly green lawn, the boys in dirty soccer gear, behind them the brick tower of the Kreuzkirche on the Hohenzollernring, the gray-blue sky.

"Daniel, why don't you say anything?" Armin asked.

"Because it's true," Daniel said.

Armin moved directly in front of him. "What's true?"

"I am one."

"One what?"

"A half-Jew."

"Excuse me? I don't believe that. I don't."

"That's how it is," Jürgen jeered.

"You're a—a non-Aryan?" Armin stammered.

"Exactly," Daniel said.

Armin shook his head. "Oh, shit," he said softly. And after a pause, "How come you didn't tell me?"

"Because you are an idiot," Jürgen remarked.

Armin turned to Jürgen and said calmly, "Keep your mouth *shut*!" Then he asked Daniel again, "How come you didn't tell me?"

Daniel said, "Well, now you know."

"I thought . . . man, I trusted you. Because we're friends."

"And now the friendship's over?"

Armin didn't answer.

At this moment Daniel walked away like a windup man, very straight, with choppy steps.

"Daniel!" Armin called after him.

Daniel crossed the entire playing field, past the track, over to the little hut beside the grandstand, and vanished into the changing room.

Soon afterward, wearing street shoes—his soccer boots in hand—he came out and went toward the exit. He didn't look back.

AT THE INTERSECTION

"HEH, STOP!"

Finally Armin caught up with him.

Daniel kept on—in the wrong direction, not down toward the Flottbeker Chaussee, but past the Kreuzkirche to the Roonstrasse.

"Wait," Armin called. "I want to talk to you! Come on, will you stop?"

"Leave me alone."

Armin grabbed him, held on. Daniel struggled to get free.

"Will you listen to me?" Armin asked.

"I don't want to anymore!"

They stood on the traffic island in the middle of the intersection. Passersby turned and looked at them.

"Yes, you'll listen," Armin said. "You're my best friend anyway. Nothing will change that."

The pedestrian signal turned red. Traffic started rushing past.

"But I'm a half-Jew," Daniel said. "You are German."

"So what? Relax." Armin looked around. "Come on, let's cross."

When the signal turned green, he pulled Daniel across the zebra-striped pavement to the forecourt of the church. They sat on one of the benches there.

Armin reached into the pockets of his soccer shorts. "Naturally, I didn't bring cigarettes," he said.

"Me neither."

Armin bent forward, looked at the stone squares on the ground. "So you're half Jewish? I don't care. I've known you for such a long time. You were never cowardly or deceitful."

Daniel also looked down at the ground.

"Why do you think I pledged blood brotherhood with you?" Armin asked. "I'm choosy that way. You're the best pal I could imagine."

They sat quietly. Then Daniel straightened up. "All the same, I'll get thrown out of the soccer league," he said.

"How come? On account of Jürgen's big mouth? He needs to learn how to make a goal."

"Not just on account of Jürgen."

"Not on my account, that's certain. And not on Coach's, either. He knows what he has in you."

Daniel shook his head. "Coach can't keep me, even if he wants to. He has no choice. All non-Aryans get thrown out. What do you think happened with Levin?"

"But he's all Jewish, not just half."

"And with Schneider?"

"He's got two left feet."

"He's a half-Jew," Daniel said. "Like me. That's why he got thrown out. And I will be too."

"Nah. You're staying."

"Man, there's no way."

"I don't believe that."

Daniel stared straight ahead, a bitter smile on his face. "It doesn't matter what you believe. I'll get cut."

"In that case, I'll quit," Armin said, determined. "We'll look for a league we can both play in."

"There's no such thing," Daniel said. "It's the same everywhere. No league takes non-Aryans. Not even Teutonia."

"How do you know that?"

"I just know. They've all kicked the non-Aryans out. If I want to keep on with soccer, I'll have to join a Jewish league."

"A what?"

"In the Jewish Sports Association."

"But those teams don't play in the Hamburg League."

"Naturally not."

"I'll join too."

"The Jewish Sports Association? Come on!"

"Sure."

"But they won't take you. They're not allowed. Because you're an Aryan."

"So what?"

"They're not allowed!"

Armin stood up and rubbed his thighs. He felt chilled from sitting still this long. He turned, watched the traffic rushing through the intersection, and said, "Man, it makes me want to puke!"

"What does?"

"The whole Thousand-Year Reich. If I can't play soccer with my best pal . . ." He started pacing back and forth, then stood still, and said to himself, "If the Führer knew about it, he wouldn't allow that kind of unfairness."

"You think not? Are you sure?"

"Yes, I'm sure," Armin said. "The Führer is on our side."

"Coach, unfortunately, is not," said Daniel.

FROM THE ALTONA BALKON I COULD SEE WHERE I'd left the jeep. A bunch of children stood around it, inspecting it from all sides and craning their necks, looking in.

I went over, walking faster when I realized I'd left the jeep unlocked and everything on the passenger seat—my briefcase with the documents and the folder with the hearings protocols.

When they saw me coming, the children retreated, respectfully letting me through. I could feel their glances on my back.

Inside the jeep everything was where it should be; they hadn't touched a thing. I kept the driver's door open and looked them in their unwashed faces. They lowered their eyes.

I rummaged around in the glove compartment. This was not a U.S. Army vehicle, but there was usually chewing gum in there. I found a pack and showed it to the children. At first they all looked at it silently. Then one of the smaller boys came toward me with his hand out. A bigger boy grabbed his shirt from behind and pulled him back.

I put a piece of gum into his hand. He said in English, "Tenk yu."

In my native tongue I asked the others, "You want some?" Immediately, their hands reached toward me. I emptied out the glove compartment. In the end the children stood around in a semicircle, a dozen boys and girls, all chewing gum.

I'd already gotten into the driver's seat when the little boy who'd first come forward said, "But you speak German!"

"Yes," I said, "I used to live here."

"Where?" he asked.

I turned my head to the west, toward the Flottbeker Chaussee. "Back there."

He asked, "Are you German?"

For a moment I didn't know what to answer.

Then I said, "No. I'm an American citizen." According to my documents, that was so.

I started the motor. But one of the bigger boys came up to the window.

"Excuse me . . . ," he began.

"What is it?"

"Could I have a cigarette?"

I looked him over. He was tall, thin, fourteen at most.

"For my father," he explained. "He loves to smoke. But we can't afford cigarettes anymore."

I took out a pack and pressed it into his hand.

Then I put the jeep in gear.

The littler ones started to wave. I waved back. I stepped hard on the gas, took off, but I could not rid my mind of that grimy little gum-chewing boy asking, *"Are you German?"*

I'd wrestled that question to the ground. And I'd settled it forever, one long-ago Sunday in autumn 1935—or so I thought. Yet here in my birthplace, ten years later, the question raised its ugly head again . . . and still had power over me.

Back then, after what happened to me during soccer practice that Wednesday afternoon, I'd been in a kind of stupor, so shocked and dazed that the full despair of it did not at first rise to consciousness.

At home I said nothing. I knew how my parents would react. My mother would have been frantic, started crying loudly. I didn't need that. So I kept quiet and hid in my room. There were three days left of fall vacation, and there was no urgent reason to leave the house.

One thing was clear: The news that I was a half-Jew would travel fast. The following Monday I'd go back to school. By then everyone I knew would know: my classmates, the teachers, the director, the Ape, probably also the saleslady in the bakery on the Mühlenstrasse. Then what would happen?

I wasn't even sure how things would be with Armin and whether he would stick to his friendship pledge. In a bitter way I was glad it was out and didn't have to be kept secret anymore. At least that's what I told myself while I stayed home for fear of running into anyone.

Then Sunday came. Our team played soccer every Sunday at eleven. The home games took place on the field near the Kreuzkirche.

That morning we played our archrival, Pinneberg . . . while I stared out my window at the Sunday promenaders strolling along the Flottbeker Chaussee.

I ached to be with my soccer team! But I knew they wouldn't let me play. I imagined staying on the sidelines where no one would see me. I just wanted to watch. I hadn't missed a game in years, even when I was only a substitute player. And now, when finally I'd been given a position, I was cut! I couldn't stand it. I had to forcibly hold myself back from running straight to the field.

I kept looking at the clock. At a quarter to twelve I could almost hear the umpire whistle for a break, and again at twelve, for halftime. Not till one o'clock, when the game would have been nearly over, did I go out.

What for, where to? I don't remember and probably did not know at the time.

Maybe to go to Armin's, find out how the game went.

But I didn't get that far. On the Königstrasse, I ran into some boys from the team: Erwin, Klaus, and a few others. Armin wasn't with them, I saw right away.

They were still in their soccer clothes. I couldn't tell by their faces how the morning had turned out. No suggestion of a rousing victory or a crushing defeat. They looked as if the game had ended in a tie.

When I saw them, I wanted to wave, say hello. But no one greeted me. They just kept going. That was all.

Erwin and Klaus had never been close friends of mine. Still, they were teammates, soccer pals. We'd played together for years. And I admired Klaus, who'd always been fair and ready to help.

Now he walked past me, just like that. With not a word. Although I knew he had seen me. The others, too. He didn't glance away or act like he hadn't noticed. He looked through me. Even so, I tried to smile. Why? None of them smiled back.

Why *did* I try to smile?

The situation was unbearably embarrassing for me—even though, as I later realized, it should have embarrassed them, too. But it didn't seem to. By smiling, I betrayed myself, and that smile was like a fire burning on my face.

I stood still on the sidewalk, and they walked on. I felt as detached as if I were the last and only person in the world. They said nothing. And that silence was worse than any insult or abuse.

I stood there and followed them with my eyes. Erwin had always had a lopsided walk. And Klaus swung his arms up and down and made fists to emphasize something he was saying.

I'm the lowest. That's how I felt. Someone you don't even greet. A nothing.

And suddenly everything that I'd been keeping at a distance burst in on me: all the fear, all the shame, all the humiliation. I just stood there, on the sidewalk, in front of some store window as people walked by me. I stood in their way, got shoved, and a short man with a hat on said, "Look out," when it was he who should have looked out.

And in that moment I knew hatred. I followed my erstwhile teammates with my eyes, and I hated every one of them. I imagined running up to the bunch, grabbing Klaus, spinning him around, letting him have it—in the face with my fist. Till the blood gushed out.

But my hand didn't hurt him. Every blow I dealt him hurt him not at all, hurt only me. It hurt so much, I tried with all my might to obliterate this scene, erase it from my mind.

But I couldn't switch off the hatred engine inside my head. I hated everybody. The coach, too. Even Armin. All the idiots in our class. The Ape. My father. My mother. Miriam—to whom I owed all of this shit. And now this little man with the hat, who banged into me saying, "Look out."

I walked mechanically. Everyone I saw, I hated. I hated the women in their Sunday clothes and the men with their round hats and walking sticks. All the small, clean children. And the SA men in uniform, who stood around at street corners. I imagined going into a weapons store, buying a revolver, loading it, and shooting them all. I imagined taking a train to Berlin, going to the Reich's ministry, and shooting Hitler and Hess and Göring. I saw their startled faces, the gaping mouths, the entry holes in their foreheads, the bright blood spurting.

And I imagined being arrested, beaten, stepped on, locked into a cell, and then, blindfolded, coming before the firing squad.

In my mind I smoked one last cigarette. And then I felt myself getting shot, felt how the bullets sliced into my body, first hot, then ripping me apart. And I knew that I'd earned it. Because my mother was a Jewess. Because I was subhuman, an animal, a parasite.

I tried to stop these imaginings. But I was invaded, enveloped by hate. I couldn't take a step or think a thought without coming up against it. The world seemed made of one huge, ravenous hatred, nothing more.

I'd walked along the entire Königstrasse to the great lawn in front of the town hall. I stood at the fountain. Little birds were bathing in it. The day was fair; the sun shone down on strollers treading the autumn leaves.

I saw only one way out. I had to get away. I didn't want to die and get buried just so that they'd all be sorry afterward. That's not what it was about.

I wanted to vanish. Never to have been.

I sank onto a bench and wallowed in the feeling of nonexistence, of dissolution, of disappearing into the balmy air. Eyes closed, I felt the sunbeams on my corneas, bursts of light exploding every which way on my retinas. And I felt that this light was inside me. It shone in the center of me. I leaned forward and opened my eyes.

I had to do something. Because, otherwise, I couldn't go on living. I had to change something in myself; to guarantee that I would never again feel like this. So small, obliterated.

I decided I was not a German anymore.

I'd been prepared to go to war and give my life for this country, this people. But that was a mistake. They didn't even want me in their soccer league.

No, I said to myself. *If I have to feel like this to get them to let me be one of them, then, no, I'd rather not. Never again will I feel so small.*

From that day on, I was no longer a German.

That was in the autumn of 1935.

PAINTING

ARMIN HAD NO INTENTION OF ABANDONING Daniel, never mind Jürgen or the others who told him he must do so.

He knew what it was like, being an outsider. He'd done well at his public elementary school and, as a gifted student, received a scholarship. The money enabled him to transfer to the exclusive Christianeum, where his schoolmates came from mostly well-to-do families. They all spoke high, proper German and thought his rough Old Altona dialect comical (he couldn't even say a clear-sounding *a!*).

They all took for granted their clean, well-ironed clothing and enjoyed thick sausage slices in their sandwiches at recess, whereas Armin's clothes, though clean, were rumpled. At best he brought along a piece of bread and butter for recess; when times were not so good, plain bread; when worse, nothing.

He came to the Christianeum at a time of the economic crisis, when many Germans were extremely poor and often went hungry. For Armin and two others from so-called socially weak families, the school kindly provided glasses of fresh milk and raisin bread.

Armin liked the raisin bread, but he hated sitting with the shoemaker's twins from the parallel class at the "asocial table." They wore thick glasses, their eyes were all blurry, and their lips drooped, drooled. They looked like half-wits, everyone agreed. But they were math geniuses. While still only in the lowest class, they breezed through problems that stumped the senior students. Armin avoided talking with them.

What he minded most were the painful collections made on his behalf before class excursions. The teacher, Dr. Schnurrbacher, would tactfully request that students from "wealthy families" (all the others) contribute an extra groschen for any student from a "socially weak family." With an extra ten pfenning, Schnurrbacher bought the bus or train ticket and inconspicuously handed it to Armin, who'd gladly have missed out on going and be spared the shame.

The winter of '32, when Armin's father lost his unemployment compensation, there wasn't money to buy even notebooks or ink. Besides, Armin caught the flu. He ran a high fever but went to school nonetheless, because he'd get something to eat there and the classrooms would be heated. At home the Hillmanns had heat for only an hour or so in the morning and evening. The rest of the time their apartment was dank and freezing cold.

Armin never talked about his home life. But Daniel had eyes, he saw, he knew. He asked his mother for extra sandwiches to bring for recess and gave them to Armin. He left blank notebooks lying on his friend's desk, without comment. Armin said they weren't his, but he ended up taking them. And at the bakery on the Mühlenstrasse where they went for *Franzbrötchen*, Daniel always paid, and Armin looked away, embarrassed.

He was determined not to be like his father. He didn't know yet what he'd be when he grew up—a soccer player, maybe, or an engineer—but one thing he did know: He'd never be out of work. He would always have enough money to buy school supplies for his boy.

Armin lived two separate lives: Mornings, he was a *Gymnasium* student, in the company of sons of rich industrialists and such; afternoons, he hung out in the courtyards and back alleys of Old Altona.

Daniel was the link between these lives, sharing in each; but even with him, there were subjects—taking charity, for instance—that Armin wouldn't, or couldn't, discuss. And so, years later, Armin couldn't hold it against his friend when it turned out that Daniel had kept the secret of being half Jewish from him.

Once the secret was out, Dr. Kammacher, director of the Christianeum, called Daniel to his office. "Your father and I were comrades in the war, you know," Kammacher said, and promised somewhat pompously, "I will hold a shielding hand over you." For the time being, Daniel remained a student there.

With one exception, the teachers treated Daniel like everybody else. Only the Ape (though he did not remeasure Daniel's skull) gave him lower marks than he gave other students for comparable work.

His classmates also let Daniel be. Sure, they were all in the HJ (except for Stefan, who had asthma). But they considered themselves sophisticated, and the smart thing now was to pay less attention to the Nuremberg Laws, which addressed the whole "Jewish question," and to concentrate on the huge excitement in the offing: the 1936 Olympic games—named by Nazi propaganda the "Games of Peace." The Führer wanted the Olympics to be glorious, a festival to show the whole world that Germany was a happy and contented land filled with happy, contented people.

The anti-Jewish posters disappeared from Hamburg and other cities. There were several half-Jews on the German Olympics team, including "blond Helen," who won the silver medal for fencing and looked like an Aryan ideal.

All eyes turned to Germany, to thrill to the grand spectacle, if not at the Berlin Olympic Stadium, then in newsreels that played and replayed the opening ceremonies. Everyone could see the French Olympic team parading past the Führer's box, with arms thrust forward, giving the Hitler salute!

Imagine the French, Germany's archenemy, saluting like that! Wasn't this proof that life here was normal now—no, better than normal—and that Germany should be respected by every country in the world?

And imagine a black man, Jesse Owens, becoming the great star of 1936. He won four gold medals for short sprinting and ran ahead of all the Aryans.

Some people, of course, claimed that Owens's success was due to bribery. But the weekly newsreels showed, beyond a doubt, that he'd simply outrun the others.

So, for the moment, racial propaganda was taken with a grain of salt. Obviously, Aryans were an excellent race; and the Germans, an admirable *Volk*. But to claim that others were subhuman seemed a bit exaggerated, didn't it?

That summer the atmosphere was international, with an emphasis on the USA. The radio played American hit songs. Armin and Daniel saw *San Francisco* and *Swing Time* at the movies. And on Saturdays they went to hear jazz in the Alster Pavilion on the Jungfernstieg in the inner city.

Peter Mehlhorn invited them and other classmates to his house (his father had a music store). They listened to Peter's records: Benny Goodman, Louis

Armstrong, Fred Astaire singing "A Fine Romance."
They felt united in their passion for this new, exciting
music and didn't care—not even Daniel, for a while—
who was Aryan, who not.

The other members of the swing clique all stayed in
the HJ. But Armin talked a lot about how stupid the
endless drills seemed to him—"Left turn," "Right
turn," "About-face," and so on—and all that stuff
about "security policing."

His troop leader, Heinz Kolinski, had twice been
left back at the public high school he attended. "As
dumb as a potato," Armin reported, "but I have to obey
him unconditionally." Regularly, Kolinski would chase
his charges through meadows and fields, this way and
that. At the command "Take cover," they had to throw
themselves in full regalia headlong into the mud.

Armin was the leader of a Jungvolk troop—ten- to
thirteen-year-old pip-squeaks called *Pimpfe*. He had to
get them to storm a hill that other *Pimpfe* were holding
and defending. The whole exercise ended in a wild
free-for-all. What was the sense of that?

He told Daniel the only reason he still went
along was that he'd soon be promoted to regular HJ
troop leader.

And then, one Sunday morning, Armin stood, shaken,
at the Kraushaars' door. He'd come straight from

night terrain maneuvers at a nearby fort. He acted panicky, refusing to tell what had happened till they were in Daniel's room, with the door shut.

There he slumped into the armchair, leaned his head back, and began.

SHOTS IN THE DARK

"TROOP LEADER KOLINSKI ORDERED US TO bring guns or revolvers, also flashlights. There were roughly one hundred of us. We pitched our tents and ate supper. Then target practice began.

"First we shot at bottles. But when it got too dark to see the bottles, Kolinski made the *Pimpfe* hold up their flashlights and started shooting at those instead. That didn't feel right to me. But he was in no mood to be reasoned with.

"At first it went smoothly. Kolinski is no genius, but he's a good shot. Then he got tired and missed. A boy fell down, but he didn't cry. The bullet only grazed his knee. We bound up the wound with bandages from the first-aid kit.

"I told Kolinski he should stop. Kolinski said no, it was the boy's own fault, for not holding the flashlight up straight. I kept on arguing. He told me to keep quiet. He's my superior, after all.

"Next, it was Hans-Dieter's turn to hold his flashlight up. He's in my Jungvolk troop. He's pretty small—actually, very small. And only twelve years old. He was tired, too, but didn't want to show it. He held up the flashlight pretty high. He tried to do it right, but he was trembling. The flashlight wobbled. Kolinski couldn't get a bead on it; he shot a little to the left. That's where Hans-Dieter's forehead was.

"The bullet made a different sound than if it had hit a tree. Hans-Dieter kind of swayed. He stayed standing a few seconds . . . then keeled over.

"We turned our flashlights on him. There was blood next to his right eye. But the hole was very small. The Red Cross boy put handkerchiefs on the wound. But the blood seeped through, so then he put moss on it. Hans-Dieter didn't talk or moan. The Red Cross boy said that was a good sign.

"After two or three hours a doctor came and said that Hans-Dieter had died the instant he was shot."

Daniel didn't know what to say. Finally he stood up and laid his hand on Armin's shoulder.

"He was dead as a doornail, that Hans-Dieter," Armin said in a low voice, and started to cry.

Daniel wanted to comfort his friend but couldn't think of anything appropriate to say.

"I'll write a complaint," Armin said, sniffling. "It won't bring little Hans-Dieter back. But that fellow Kolinski should get what's coming to him."

Daniel remembered stories he'd heard about how

tough the HJ was, not like kindergarten, that's for sure. Armin had told a few such stories himself. But not about anyone dying.

"You'll complain? To whom?" Daniel asked.

"To the Reich youth leader," Armin said.

Daniel had never heard of anybody doing that, nor of an HJ leader getting reprimanded for doing anything wrong.

Armin did write his complaint. He was that outraged. But what happened next made him even angrier. Because nothing happened. Kolinski was transferred to head some other troop, that was it.

And the Gestapo took Hans-Dieter's father away; he vanished—because he had dared to protest.

An obituary in the newspaper read only: *Our dear son Hans-Dieter suffered a mishap while serving the Fatherland.*

A mishap! Armin went to the company commander, who thought Kolinski had done nothing so very wrong. Armin contradicted him.

Shortly thereafter he was summoned to appear before the HJ district leader in his office in the National Socialist Party's headquarters building in the inner city. This man was second only to the Reich youth leader and had command over all HJ divisions throughout the entire district of Schleswig-Holstein. His name was Blohm.

MY HONOR MEANS LOYALTY, I
(SS MOTTO)

ARMIN GAVE BLOHM THE HITLER GREETING.
The man casually returned it and continued leafing
through a file.

Armin knew how one behaved with somebody
like that. He stayed at attention near the door, studying the golden oak leaves on Blohm's epaulets.

"'Date of entry into the HJ . . . ,'" the Reich district leader read aloud from the file.

My file, Armin realized.

Blohm read on: "'Special distinctions: promotion
to Jungvolk troop leader.' Now problems: 'Contradicts
his superiors, exhibits cowardly behavior—'"

"The allegation that I'm cowardly is unjustified."
Armin bit his lip, grew burning hot at having been so
forward.

Blohm said nothing, just gave him a long look and
asked, "Kindly describe the entire incident exactly as
you saw it."

Armin had not expected this. Neither the company

commander nor anyone else had been willing to hear him out.

Blohm stood leaning against the side of his desk, listening attentively.

When Armin was done, Blohm closed the file, sat down at the desk, and nodded. "A tragic event. I understand you're upset." He sounded earnest, sympathetic. "But that doesn't give you the right to contradict your superior."

"No, sir, Herr District Leader," Armin said.

"You might think that under the circumstances what I'm about to say is insensitive." Blohm stood up, started pacing back and forth. "But listen: When you're planing wood, there must be shavings. We're building a new Germany now. That little HJ boy's death is regrettable. But we must train our youth to grow as hard as steel. Today's HJ will all be soldiers someday, dodging bullets as they whiz by. Then will they tremble, when it's their turn to shoot? In wartime you'll experience far more drastic situations."

"But, sir, I felt pity for him," Armin said.

"Pity? The Third Reich has no room for such extravagant sentiments. It's possible that the shooting exercise was senseless. It's also possible that your superior is as stupid as an ox. Nonetheless, it's still your damned duty to be unwavering in your loyalty to him."

"Yes, sir, Herr District Leader."

"But I didn't summon you here to tell you that," said Blohm, standing directly in front of Armin. He pressed his lips together. "You were brought to my attention quite some time ago. Your achievements in the HJ have been outstanding. Your Jungvolk leadership is exemplary. And the fact that you were arrested before the power seizure for spreading forbidden propaganda . . ." Blohm smiled. "That makes you an 'old warrior,' so to speak."

Again Armin felt burning hot, but this time with pride. He'd had no idea that his night in jail back then had found its way into his file.

"You're extremely intelligent, not just an ordinary tagalong," Blohm went on. "We need your kind. But that intelligence of yours also puts you in danger. You see, somebody like your troop leader . . ."

"Kolinski," Armin said.

"Right. Someone like that is oblivious to the possibility that he did wrong. He wants to try that sort of target practice because he saw it done somewhere. To him, it's a test of courage, that's all. He hasn't given it a thought and doesn't even remember that poor little *Pimpf*. But you're different. You do think about such things. That is to your credit—but it's a failing, too. You must be careful not to think too much." Blohm made a fist. "What counts in the end is action. Sometimes you have to turn off your intelligence and simply act. Do you understand me?"

"Yes, sir, Herr District Leader," Armin said.

"I'd just as soon promote you to HJ troop leader today rather than tomorrow," Blohm said. "However . . ."

He turned back to the desk and leafed through Armin's file again, looking pensive, frowning. "You really don't make it easy for me."

Of course not, thought Armin, and knew what was coming.

"You're still in close touch with a non-Aryan," said Blohm.

"He's only half Jewish," Armin said. "And in his case it's clear that the German, Aryan half is the more important half of him."

Blohm smiled, shaking his head. "How can you judge? Are you a specialist in that area?"

"No, but I know him. He's been my best friend for years."

"Yes, of course," said Blohm. "And that makes him quite different from the rest of the Jews. Listen, just about every German knows a 'good' Jew like that. But, seriously, we can't allow such friendships to exist. The truth is, Jews have no honor."

Armin wanted to argue but knew he'd better not, because Blohm's benign expression had changed. He seemed in the grip of a strong, quite personal repugnance. "I'll try to bear in mind that you are very young," he said, taking a deep breath, "that you grew up in a period when Jews no longer had much say in Germany. And so you never learned what they are really like. But you're such a bright fellow, you can surely understand how viciously world Jewry maligns us—in America, in France, everywhere. World Jewry has one goal: to destroy Germany. And every Jew in Germany, your friend included, is part of world Jewry. They all work together, conspiring against us."

Armin gathered up his courage and said, "Not all Jews are subhuman, though."

Blohm laughed briefly, with his mouth closed. "How did our propaganda minister phrase it? Certainly the Jews are people too, just as the louse is an animal—only not an agreeable one. The louse is a parasite. And whoever is beset by parasites, if he takes care of them, makes them his friends, does great harm. Not only to himself. If you have lice, here's what to do: Find them and squash them between your fingernails."

He turned away, closed Armin's file, laid it aside, and said, "I think we've discussed everything. That friendship has to stop, at once. Is that understood?"

Armin swallowed.

"Understood?" Blohm asked again in a loud, sharp voice.

"Yes, sir, Herr District Leader," Armin stammered.

"Good. Dismissed." Blohm busied himself with other papers on his desk.

Armin said, *"Heil Hitler,"* and left.

When he got downstairs and stood on the Jungfernstieg, where people crowded past him, he felt dizzy. He couldn't just go to the *S-Bahn* station and take the next train to Altona as though nothing had happened. Thoughts raced through his head as he went around the Binnenalster and through the Colonnades to the Dammtor.

What should he do? Give up his friendship with Daniel? He hadn't exactly said he would, only "Yes, sir" in answer to whether he understood. . . . And if he didn't, what would happen? Would he end up getting thrown out of the Hitler Jugend? He tried to slow these thoughts down, consider them calmly.

One thing was clear: If he got expelled from the HJ, he'd have no future in the Third Reich. And when he finished at the Christianeum, that would be the end of his education, too. . . . Merely thinking that far ahead brought on the dizziness again.

Armin reached the Dammtor station just as the train was approaching. When it stopped, he caught sight of a girl behind the glass-paned door inside the train he was about to enter. She was holding a bundle of notebooks and books.

He forgot about everything. This girl was breathtaking. True, her hair was black, but that was what he liked so much. The train door opened, she got out, they looked at each other. In a flash he knew: He'd seen her at the Kraushaars'. She was Daniel's cousin, Miriam. They both had to smile. Now he wasn't sure if she had recognized him too. The passengers behind her pushed forward, she passed him, not saying anything. But for a split second her body almost touched his, and he reeled as though struck by lightning.

PESTILENCE

SOPHIE SMILED, LOOKING OUT THE WINDOW as the train sped past the Dutch border. They were leaving Germany! Only for a short vacation. Still, she felt a heavy load lifting from her. They were abroad! In a democratic country with no swastika flags flying from the houses, no uniformed SA or SS men on the streets.

They were four in the compartment: Sophie, Rheinhard, Miriam, Daniel. It was the Kraushaars' first vacation trip in four years. Before, they'd always traveled, to the Alps in winter, or to the sea in summer. For 1934 they'd planned a trip to northern Italy but hadn't gone, and after that they hadn't made plans anymore.

But this year, 1937, Rheinhard had to go to Amsterdam on business, and since the trip would coincide with Easter vacation, he mentioned the idea to his wife. Sophie was surprised, delighted, even though it was to be only for one week.

The family hiked, went to the seashore, and rested,

enjoying the spring air and freedom from the strains they'd been under.

They saw *Don Carlos* at the German theater in Amsterdam, with well-known actors banned in Germany. When the rebel Marquis of Posa spoke the line, "Above all, sire, grant freedom of thought," the audience applauded.

There were quite a few Germans in this city— refugees, clearly. Sophie envied them. She longed to emigrate. And Daniel had changed his mind about it; he wanted to emigrate now. But to Rheinhard, the idea remained abhorrent.

In a café they got into a conversation with an elderly couple who had left Germany before 1933. The husband admitted that now they were plagued with homesickness. This news strengthened Rheinhard's resolve never to flee his native land. But at least he and Sophie didn't quarrel about it while they were on vacation.

The trip back was not pleasant. Sophie felt like a prisoner being returned to jail after a failed escape attempt. The family's week away made the prospect of what lay ahead seem even worse. As they approached the border she saw that certain "German look," nervous glances left and right on other passengers' faces, and knew she wore it too.

A pestilence has broken out, a terrible disease, and

no one has noticed, Sophie thought. *It has infected everyone, and now it's an epidemic. . . .*

Once home in Hamburg, Sophie bought herself a notebook and, for the first time since her girlhood, kept a diary. But she didn't write down self-reflections as she had then. She noted all the little symptoms, some scarcely discernible, that characterized the sickness: the excuses neighbors found to avoid one another, the reputed successes of the regime, the rationalizations people thought up for what the Nazis were doing. Someone Rheinhard knew compared wearing the swastika armband to wearing a Red Cross carnation on Armistice Day. Yes, the armband was embarrassing, but luckily, you didn't have to wear it all the time, only on special occasions.

Sophie noted how scared people were, even of their own telephones, in which they suspected sneaky listening devices might be hidden to record not just phone conversations but every word spoken in the room. And nobody did anything about it! No, people accepted being afraid. They grew used to it—and this seemed to Sophie even worse. They stopped noticing the symptoms of the sickness, started to forget that things hadn't always been like that. Criminals, murderers were governing the country, and the people cheered for them. Surely nowhere else would the citizenry hold still for that monkey with the mustache ranting and screaming. And in this land he had more power than any previous ruler ever had.

It was as though the Germany she'd known had vanished. No, worse—as though it had decided to obliterate itself. The strength and the spirit that had once created art, poetry, and science were now spent creating the worst of all possible worlds.

Often when Sophie thought about these things, the words to "The Wanderer," her favorite Schubert song, pulsed through her head:

> *Where are you, my beloved land?*
> *Land so hopeful and so green,*
> *Land in which my roses bloom,*
> *Where my good friends go wandering,*
> *And where my dead will rise again,*
> *Land that speaks my native tongue,*
> *Oh Land, where can you be?*

Soon after returning from Holland, Sophie found out where Sebastian had been sent: to Fuhlbüttel, the former prison, now a concentration camp. As his sister, she had permission to go there once a week, to bring clean clothes, a small food parcel, and take away his dirty laundry, but, naturally, not to visit him. She could go no farther than the guardhouse at the entrance. At least she knew that he was still alive. They let her leave a letter for him and receive one from him—carefully written, because, naturally all such letters were opened and read by censors.

Rheinhard wasn't happy about her trips to Fuhlbüttel, but he did not prevent them.

He was earning less from clients these days. A tacit boycott had begun. So, for the first time since the 1920s, the family had money worries. Matters were still not critical, but they had to be careful about expenditures which, before, they would have made without hesitation.

And something else was different too. Until now the family had been "protected," so to speak, thanks to Rheinhard being Aryan and having good connections. That they could no longer count on this luxury became unmistakably clear on, as it happened, the 6th of July, a date of great significance to Rheinhard.

TRENCHES

IT WAS ON JULY 6 THAT RHEINHARD HAD BEEN awarded the Iron Cross.

On the anniversary of that day, therefore, he never went to the office. Generally quite unsentimental, he observed July 6 as others did their birthdays, because, as he often said, on that day his life was given to him for the second time.

Daniel learned early that the sixth was special because his father, usually so silent, so unwilling to let himself be known, was different on that date each year. He allowed Daniel to watch when he brought out the box in which he kept his medals: the Iron Cross and another, simpler-looking one. Also, the metal identification tag from when he'd joined the army in 1914 and a yellowed newspaper clipping from 1917 showing a photo taken at the front. Somewhere in the background of that photo, almost unrecognizable, was Rheinhard's face.

On July 6, every year since, Rheinhard pinned his Iron Cross on his suit jacket. And in the evening he would take Daniel on his lap and tell stories from the "Great War."

Daniel always waited in suspense for the one about the Iron Cross. Because every year Rheinhard added new details—details that, the year before, Daniel would have been too young to hear, since they were too upsetting and he wouldn't have understood. When he first heard the story, at age six, all he'd learned was that his father fought in the 1914–1918 war, which, thank God, was over now, and that his father had been brave, gone into the enemy's trenches, and had received the Iron Cross for doing so. There was no mention then of anyone wounded or killed and certainly no mention of getting buried alive.

Once Daniel started school, he heard all sorts of bloody war stories and found out that noncommissioned officers got the Iron Cross only if they had done something extraordinary and had suffered serious injury. He asked his father to tell him more. So Rheinhard told him that of the two comrades on patrol with him, one had died—though not how it happened, only that the poor fellow hadn't paid attention in a crucial moment. This judgment led to a long lecture about how Daniel, now that he was going to school on his own, had to be very careful and pay strict attention to everything along the way.

That night, in bed, Daniel had stayed awake trying hard to imagine things that his father had left out of the story.

Gradually, year by year, he found out more, and he always wished Rheinhard would tell it all.

Before the age of twelve this is what Daniel knew: His father and two comrades had volunteered for night patrol. They stole across the front line. The two comrades held their revolvers to a French lookout's back while Rheinhard snatched his rifle away. Then they entered an enemy trench.

They were discovered while exploring. But it was a very dark night. And the French were sure they'd climb out and make a run for it. So they aimed their shots midway between their own and the German lines. Rheinhard and his comrades outsmarted them by waiting out the salvos down in the trench. And they continued to explore, noting positions to tell to the German grenade throwers later.

Around four in the morning they slipped back. They got to within twenty-five meters of their own trenches when a German mine exploded directly in front of them. Unable to go forward, they crept into a nearby dugout the French had abandoned. It had dead soldiers in it, as well as some severely wounded who clung to life, moaning softly.

Rheinhard and his comrades lay in this dugout the whole day. In case a French patrol appeared, they were prepared to pick them off one by one as the enemy entered the narrow passageway.

The three were gone for twenty-seven hours.

At nightfall they sneaked the rest of the way to the German lines! Their company commander invited them to dine. He presented them to the battalion commander and even the brigadier general, to whom they reported their significant military observations.

Finally, when Daniel turned twelve, he found out about that other medal of his father's, not the Iron Cross, but the one for getting buried alive.

Rheinhard tried to make it sound quite harmless: When that mine had exploded in front of them, big chunks of earth had spurted up. Some landed on top of them, and they couldn't get out from under. Not right away. Luckily, though, Rheinhard was able to dig, and after a while he worked his way free.

Daniel didn't find out what really happened till the year he was thirteen. And he started to understand at last why his father sometimes cried out in the night and couldn't go back to sleep and sat and read in the living room till morning.

That mine had ripped one of his father's comrades apart. Schultheiss was his name. He and Rheinhard had both stood up, Schultheiss first, so he was the one it shattered, and his torn-off limbs came flying at Rheinhard. . . .

On July 6, 1933, with the Nazis newly in power and Rheinhard so downhearted, he could no longer hold back this part of the story.

The chunks of earth had buried them. His father had lost consciousness.

When he came to, he lay crumpled in total blackness, squeezed in by earth on all sides. His head was pressed between his legs—and right there, it so happened, was a bit of a hollow with air in it, enabling him to breathe.

Of course he tried to stand up, but the earth that held him trapped was too deep, and he couldn't budge it.

"So then," and now he told it, "I took leave of my life. I fell for the Fatherland"—a thought that gave him comfort. He gasped for air, felt glowing hot, and fought with all his strength to stand—but he couldn't. In minutes the oxygen would be used up. And that would be the end.

Lying there so painfully cramped, he made one last quite different attempt: He pressed one foot downward, hoping that would propel him up. He turned the foot, dug down with it . . . and suddenly inched forward, which slightly improved his position, for now he could raise his head a little and press it against the earth.

The earth gave way, one millimeter or two, but that enabled him to free his hand, reach up, press hard, push and push, and turn and push and turn again. And, yes, it was working. He heard bits of earth trickling past his ear. He'd made a hollow space to poke his head into. He kept on turning his hand, twisting it upward. And suddenly the hand was free. He felt the air around it. He pulled his hand back, then he breathed—yes, breathed!—the air that streamed into the hole along with the bits of earth that skidded down.

He dug with both his hands now, widening the hole so he could get his head into the open, then his upper body, and finally squeeze his whole self through.

Outside it was already dusk, only a thin stripe of sunlight still on the horizon. He looked around, taking deep, deep breaths, thinking, *Now there's nothing left to do but return to my unit. . . .* But then he remembered Schultheiss, ripped apart, and the other comrade still buried down there. So Rheinhard kept digging till he got the man free. He was unconscious. Rheinhard pulled him up, hoisted him across his back, and crawled, on all fours, the darkening distance to the German position.

This story, which Daniel heard in July of 1933, was the last version Rheinhard told.

In the years that followed, his father and many other veterans who had not joined the Nazi party wore their Iron Crosses more and more often, in order to prove that they had a right to exist still, as Rheinhard once wryly remarked.

His ritual of honoring the July 6 date lost more and more of its meaning. He stayed home from the office. And in the evening they went to the theater or to a concert. But once the Nuremberg Laws went into effect, this was no longer possible. They had to make do with going to the cinema.

Naturally, even that was FORBIDDEN TO JEWS, as the large sign proclaimed at the entrance to the movie house. But it said nothing about mixed-marriage spouses or their children. In any case, nobody objected to their presence. And so, on July 6, 1937, the Kraushaar family went to the Royal in the Papenstrasse.

A film with Zarah Leander was showing. The cinema was nearly sold out. But they were lucky and got good seats in the first row of the balcony. They made themselves comfortable. The weekly newsreel began. Then an usher approached and timidly requested that they leave.

Rheinhard asked, "What do you mean?"

The usher pointed to the entrance. There stood a gentleman and lady. The gentleman was a well-known Nazi official. He had his eye on their seats.

Outraged, Rheinhard refused to budge. They had purchased their tickets. No, he said, leaving the cinema was out of the question. The usher turned away.

Then the manager came. He spoke to Rheinhard,

retreated to the Party official, came back again, and "regretfully" requested that the four of them vacate their seats, and so on. The entire audience turned to observe the scene.

The manager made it clear that they would be removed by force if necessary. The Kraushaars stood up and left.

THROWN OUT

WHEN DANIEL WAS YOUNGER, HE'D NEVER seen his parents quarrel. Rheinhard was a strong believer in maintaining self-control. Certainly there'd been times of tension between him and Sophie, but they didn't air their differences in front of their son.

On rare occasions when they thought he'd left the house or was upstairs asleep, he'd overheard them argue, though always with restraint. Sometimes he wished they'd just let loose and have it out.

Now they did, more and more—or rather, his mother let loose. Trying to break through his father's stony silence, she'd provoke a quarrel and always ended up in tears.

Her nerves were frazzled, and no wonder. Insults, obscenities came almost daily in the mail. One letter— anonymous, of course—contained a single, one-way ticket to Jerusalem! And often when the phone rang, it was somebody unknown uttering a slur, then hanging up. And children marked up the sidewalk in front of the Kraushaars' door, chalking JEWS in big white letters. One time they drew a gallows, too.

All of which brought Sophie near the breaking point. So did the vicious Jew-hating headlines at kiosks and Goebbels and Hitler orating on the radio. Daniel and Rheinhard couldn't understand why she wouldn't just turn it off. No, she had to listen, hard, to every word. And afterward she'd be distraught for hours.

Days when she went to "visit" Sebastian were the worst.

But ordinary things upset her also: Rheinhard coming home late, keeping supper waiting; a letter left lying where it didn't belong; a key that couldn't be found; or Rheinhard not answering when she asked him a question. His silences could drive her mad.

"Am I married to a deaf-mute?" she'd burst out. Next thing, she'd be in tears. Then she'd bring up emigrating and say things, like "I can't stand it here anymore! You won't leave! And it's destroying me!"

Normally, Daniel stayed out of the way if his parents were in the living room with tension in the air. But one day he had to pass through to the library to get a book he needed for a homework assignment on Greek architecture. *"Hallo,"* he said, but they took no notice of him.

Rheinhard sat in his armchair, leafing through a law journal. Sophie stood behind him at the window, gazing at the brown leaves of a potted plant on the sill.

"Tell me, was it you who overwatered the plants?" she asked, sounding as though something dreadful had happened.

Rheinhard kept staring at the journal. He'd been even more silent than usual for the past few days.

"Would you please answer me when I ask you a question?" Sophie said.

Here we go again, Daniel thought. The clock said ten past five. On most days there'd already been at least one crying jag by then. He hurried into the library.

"Go on, tell me what's wrong," he heard Sophie say.

"What should be wrong?" Rheinhard asked.

Daniel turned to the bookcase.

At Rheinhard's insistence, the books were arranged alphabetically by authors' names, not by subject matter. But Daniel knew of no particular author, so he had to search shelf after shelf to find what he was looking for.

"I can sense there's something wrong," he heard Sophie saying. "You go to the office, you come home and don't say a word, don't want to hear from anyone or see anyone, you treat your family as though we're not here . . ."

"I'm just not feeling very talkative," Rheinhard answered.

"All right, *don't* talk. Be secretive," Sophie muttered. "I give up."

Daniel heard her steps come nearer, then she appeared in the library doorway. He had just found the book on his subject and pulled it off the shelf. She started when she saw him.

"Oh, you're here?"

"As you can see. I was just about to go upstairs."

She moved her head in the direction of the living room and said, loud enough for Rheinhard to hear, "He's playing deaf-mute again."

Then she called to her husband, "Why don't you go to the office if our company is so unpleasant?"

She turned back to Daniel, shrugging.

After a moment's silence Rheinhard said, "I don't go to the office because he threw me out."

Sophie and Daniel stood as if frozen. Then, slowly, Sophie turned back into the living room.

Rheinhard had spoken clearly. Nevertheless, she asked, "What did you say?"

Rheinhard answered, "Karl fired me. He threw me out of my own law practice."

Now Daniel joined his parents in the living room. Rheinhard sat in the armchair, still holding the law journal in his hands. Suddenly his face seemed old and worn.

Sophie looked stunned. "But that can't be."

"Yes," said Rheinhard, "it decidedly can."

Only now did Sophie and Daniel learn that the law practice had not belonged to Rheinhard for over a year. Under massive pressure, he had signed a document transferring ownership to his associate, Karl. In order that the practice might continue.

"Why didn't you say a word about it?" Sophie asked.

Rheinhard only lifted up his hands.

"Today I had to clear out my office," he said, trying to sound matter-of-fact. "I was permitted to pack up my 'personal effects.' . . . And my old assistant Dorfler showed me out. As though I wouldn't have found my own way!"

Rheinhard sat there sunken into himself. "When I first took Karl on, he was fresh out of school, still wet behind the ears. Not a penny in his pockets, no idea how he would feed his family. So I made him my associate. He was a nobody."

Rheinhard shook his head. "And now he throws me out. 'Be reasonable, Rheinhard. There's no other way. The Justice Ministry insists . . .'"

Rheinhard sat up and looked at Sophie. "Now Karl takes over the practice," he continued, his voice strengthening. "It was me the clients came to for a strong defense. And now this weakling will defend them. In truth, he's a bad lawyer. That's what's so appalling. I just now realized it. I'd kept thinking he was still young, still had a lot to learn. . . . But now he's not so young anymore. And he has learned nothing. An opportunist without talent taking over my practice!"

He shook his head angrily, as though this were the most awful thing about the whole story. "I should have suspected it when he joined the Party. But I was so trusting. . . . 'A mere formality,' he'd said, and claimed he found it disagreeable. 'But nowadays, if one wants to get ahead . . .'"

Sophie stared into space. "He has caught the pestilence," she said. "The pestilence that's broken out and no one noticed."

Daniel stood with the book in his hand.

In the middle of this silence the doorbell rang. No one stirred.

When it rang again, Sophie walked stiffly and somehow too slowly into the foyer.

Daniel and Rheinhard heard her opening the door, asking, "What do you want?"

Before the reply came, Sophie let out a shriek, then started crying, loudly. Daniel ran to the foyer, Rheinhard following.

RETURN

IT WAS DARK IN THE FOYER. SOPHIE HELD someone in an embrace, a man in a gray coat. His arms hung slackly by his sides. Sophie stopped sobbing and called out, "Oh, God . . ."

Daniel moved to his mother's side. From there he could see the man's shaved head. The man was crying. Although he looked not at all like Daniel's uncle Sebastian, something about his emaciated, grayish face reminded Daniel of him. And he realized that was who it had to be.

Sophie stepped back, then took her brother by the arm and led him into the living room, slowly, as though leading someone who was ill. When she got him there, she took off his hat and helped him with his coat.

Rheinhard came toward him and reached out his hand. He held Sebastian's hand in his for a long while and finally said, "Welcome."

"Thank you." Sebastian looked anxiously around. "And Miriam—?"

"She's well. She's at her Hebrew lesson," Sophie said, and asked her brother, "Are you hungry? Would you like something to drink? Tea? Maria will have the kettle on." She hurried downstairs to the kitchen.

"Tea would be nice," Sebastian said softly, as though to himself.

Rheinhard eased him into a chair and smiled at him. "You're back . . . and well."

"Halfway," Sebastian murmured, then, to Daniel, "You've grown tall."

"Yes," Daniel answered.

Sophie came back in with a small tray, put it down on the sideboard, and poured Sebastian a cup of tea.

Rheinhard handed it to him. "Milk and sugar?"

"Yes, why not?" Sebastian said.

Sophie handed him the sugar bowl. He took one lump. Then he drank without stirring.

"So this is how it is," he said when he'd put the cup down. "Outside. With you." He picked up the cup again, did not drink, but covered it with his free hand as though to warm himself. Finally he smiled and said, "Tea with sugar."

"Yes, that still exists," Rheinhard said, "though it's sometimes a bit hard to get."

Sebastian emptied his cup and looked up. "Yes, and you?" he asked. "Is everything all right with you?"

Rheinhard pursed his lips and lifted a hand, indicating that there was too much to tell in just a few sentences.

Sophie had not taken her eyes off Sebastian. "Everything's all right with us all," she said. "More or less."

"Normal life," Rheinhard said, smiling.

Sebastian bent forward, set the cup on the table, and asked, "When will Miriam be back from the Hebrew lesson?"

Sophie checked the time: a few minutes past four. "Soon. She'll be back soon."

"COINCIDENCE"

ARMIN STOOD BEHIND THE KIOSK AND READ the headlines for the third time, then looked over to the entrance of the building again. It was a quarter past four, and still no Miriam.

Her classmates had already come out, one by one, so as not to arouse any suspicion about what they did up there on the third floor.

Finally the dark, heavy door opened again. Even before he saw her face, Armin recognized her dark blue dress.

And even though he'd been planning for weeks to "accidentally" run into her, he asked himself at this moment, *What am I really after?* Since their meeting at the Dammtor *S-Bahn* station he hadn't stopped thinking of her. Yet now, once he saw her with the notebooks and books under her arm, his plan seemed totally insane.

A minute ago he couldn't wait to see her, speak to her. But now he hid behind the kiosk, not knowing if he should.

How many times had he imagined this meeting? *Usually I'm not so shy,* he thought. *Why now?* He didn't understand it. All he knew was, he wanted to know this girl better. . . .

She came down the few steps to the street. She didn't turn right, toward the small basement café on the next street. But why? She'd had a hot chocolate there last week after the lesson. Armin had followed her, then hadn't dared to go in. He'd decided that today he would—but she headed left. Another second and she'd have crossed the street and boarded the streetcar.

Armin started running.

Just as she was about to step off the sidewalk they almost collided. No other way could he have stopped her.

"Look out!" she cried, dropping a notebook. She bent down to retrieve it. He did too. Again they nearly collided.

They both straightened up. Armin handed her the notebook and muttered an excuse.

"What for? It was nothing," she said.

They stood facing each other. He thought, *If she doesn't recognize me now* . . . just as she said: "Listen . . . I know you from somewhere."

Armin had to grin.

"You're a friend of Daniel's, aren't you?"

"Yes." Armin tried to look casual.

She narrowed her eyes and said, "Anton, or something like that . . ."

"Armin, to be exact. And you're his cousin, right? Miriam."

She nodded.

"I'm sorry about just now—"

"Nonsense," she said.

He could have stood there forever. And it seemed to him not necessary to say anything more. Just to stand facing her like that, at the edge of the sidewalk . . .

But that wasn't possible. She was already looking to see if the next streetcar was coming. He had to say something, and quickly. So he asked, "What do you do here?" Even though he knew the answer.

"Piano lesson," she said.

He liked that, even though it wasn't true. He'd always wanted to know a girl who took piano lessons. Besides, he took the lie as some sort of proof that she, too, was not indifferent to their meeting.

RENDEZVOUS

MIRIAM FELT FAIRLY SURE THAT ARMIN knew the reason she came to that building. She didn't really understand why she had lied. Probably because she wouldn't have enjoyed talking with him about Hebrew lessons. It wasn't the easiest of topics.

Armin asked if he could walk her home.

"Not necessary," Miriam said. "I'm taking the streetcar. It's too far, on foot."

"Then I'll walk you to the streetcar stop," he said.

Miriam had to laugh. "It's just there."

"Oh, right." He sounded disappointed.

They stood opposite each other for a moment. Then he asked, "Listen . . . have you got time, I mean, just a little?"

"What for?"

"How about if we go to a café? Back there, I know a nice one."

"Do you sometimes go there?" she asked.

"Yes. I thought . . . Would you like a hot chocolate? On me? As my apology."

"Hmm . . ." She considered. She often went there after Hebrew. It made her feel like a normal girl to sit someplace and have a hot chocolate. The couple who owned the café seemed friendly, and the NO JEWS sign hung in a dark corner where you almost couldn't see it. Going there was dangerous, but worth it.

"Well, why not?"

And now I'm going there with someone in the HJ, Miriam thought. And later she wondered, *How come I never suspected that it might not have been by "coincidence," our bumping into each other like that?*

Armin talked nonstop, about soccer.

Actually, he should have been at soccer practice right then. But his knee still hurt from an injury that he described to her in lively detail.

After a while it occurred to him that he should ask her about something. So he asked what she thought— about soccer.

"Well," Miriam answered, "twenty-two players chasing after a ball . . ."

"Twenty chasers," he corrected her. "Two stand in the goals."

"That doesn't make it better."

"Did you ever play?"

"Nah."

"Then you shouldn't be so quick to criticize it," he said. "Soccer is the best. When you're running with the ball . . . and you fake out your opponent . . . go

201

storming to the goal . . . you kick, and the ball lands smack in the corner . . ." He stopped and gazed into the distance. "It's such a rush, like a delirium. It makes you oblivious to everything that's happening around you. The feeling's magnificent."

"Sounds like a drug," said Miriam.

"That's what it is. I have a soccer addiction. If I don't get my daily dose, I go crazy."

"Like one of those morphine addicts in films?"

"Yes, like that."

"So how do you stand it now that you can't play?"

"Who says I can stand it?"

They reached the café and went in.

As usual, it was almost empty. They sat in the back, across from each other, and now he couldn't think what else to say. Miriam couldn't either. He studied the flower pattern on the wallpaper; she thought about the innovations in Hebrew grammar that Dr. Weizmann had explained today.

Then their hot chocolate came. It was really so hot, they had to stir it for a couple of minutes. Then they drank it, and then they left.

They walked side by side, still silent.

When she stopped in front of a ladies' clothing store window, he asked, "Which of those dresses do you like?"

"None," she answered truthfully.

He cleared his throat. "Listen . . ."

"What?"

"Do you . . . do you have a boyfriend?"

Miriam looked hard at him. "Do I have what?"

"A boyfriend. Are you going with someone? Steady?"

"Am I going with someone? What kind of question is that?"

"Well, er . . ."

"Why would you want to know that?"

"Because . . ."

They walked on.

"What about you?" she asked.

He shook his head. "Nah."

"Me neither," she said.

They reached the streetcar stop, stood off to the side.

He cleared his throat again, then struggled to form a sentence: "Because I thought that, if you . . . and I, if you could imagine that we both, together . . . that we could get together and talk . . ." He looked up and met her gaze.

Miriam said, "Wait a moment. What are you saying? We don't even know each other."

"Right. Not yet," he said like a schoolboy who'd given the wrong answer. Somehow she felt sorry for him.

Meantime, the number 27 had pulled in. Miriam

knew that another one would come along in a few minutes. She kept standing to the side while everyone got on. Then she said in a low voice, "I'm Jewish. I hope you know that."

"Naturally," he said.

"So aside from everything else, how could it be? I'm not even allowed to sit on a park bench, much less sit on one with you. Didn't you ever hear of the Nuremberg Laws?"

"Sure, of course."

"So?"

New passengers were arriving, and she pulled him farther along the sidewalk.

He started another sentence. "I . . . I don't care about the Nuremberg Laws. And everything else, either. Miriam, I want . . ."

"You want what?"

"Us to get to know each other."

"But how? It doesn't make sense."

The noise of a big truck driving past cut into their conversation.

"I could meet you again," Armin ventured. "Next week. Same time, same place. After your piano lesson."

"What piano lesson?" she asked.

"The Hebrew piano lesson," he said.

"Right. You knew—"

"That you're studying Hebrew? Yes, I knew. From Daniel."

"You knew I was lying!"

He nodded.

"Why didn't you say something?" Now she felt angry. "Then it wasn't a coincidence, and you didn't just happen to be passing by?"

"Nah." He stared at the ground like a child caught misbehaving. "Definitely not a coincidence."

"Then what was it?"

"Intention."

"What did you say?"

She suddenly had to smile. He too. They stood facing each other and laughed.

"Intention?" she asked. "Our near collision on the sidewalk? And that whole what-are-you-doing-here business? That was all intentional? You were play-acting with me?"

"Yes." He nodded.

"You lured me into that café under false pretenses?"

"Yes."

"What for?"

He shrugged. How to explain? "I'd been thinking so long about how I could meet you. . . ."

"You know where I live. Why didn't you just come over?"

"I wanted to meet just you."

"Why? So you could ask if I'm 'going with' somebody or if I'm still available?"

"Yes."

The next streetcar pulled in. "I have to go," she said.

"What about next week?" he asked. "Will we see each other?"

"I don't know."

"Same time, same place?"

"What good will it do?"

"What harm will it do?"

"I have to get on this streetcar."

She ran, climbed on, and stood up front by the doors where he could see her.

"All right?" He sounded full of hope. "I'll wait for you?"

The doors closed. What should she say? She shook her head, but at the same time she smiled; she couldn't help it.

And when the streetcar started moving, she went to a window, quick. He followed her with his eyes. She didn't mean to, but her hand raised itself and waved to him. He was waving too.

"THE LORELEY"

IN AUTUMN OF 1937, AFTER RECUPERATING
at the Kraushaars' for a time, Sebastian rented a room
in the Grindelallee. He found a part-time job nearby,
in a small Jewish bookstore. His work consisted of
packing all the now forbidden volumes into crates, to
be shipped to New York, to a German-language bookstore whose owner had offered to buy them for a
laughably low price.

And Miriam told the family she would be moving
to a Zionist training camp in Rissen, in preparation for
emigrating to Palestine.

Daniel marveled at how sad he felt. When she
first came, he'd hated her, out of fear that by being so
Jewish, she'd expose him and he wouldn't be able to
hide anymore. And now how he'd miss her! She was
the one person in the house he could have good conversations with. *How will I stand it,* he thought, *when
it's just me and my parents again?*

Not that he and Miriam needed to talk all the
time. When they went for walks together, along the

Elbe to Teufelsbrück, or sometimes all the way to
Blankenese, they could pursue their own thoughts,
exchanging only a few words now and then, yet feel
perfectly at ease in each other's company.

And now she wanted to move out, live in that
training camp.

Daniel thought back to the day he'd come home early
from school, and there she'd sat, at the breakfast table:
Miriam, his cousin, quite grown up, quite pretty—and
so unmistakably Jewish, he'd wished she'd disappear
as suddenly as she had come.

That was almost two and a half years ago now,
but it seemed as far removed as if it had happened on
another planet, in another galaxy. Things had been so
different then. . . . He was still in the soccer club, as a
substitute player who saw action only after halftime.
He was fifteen, sneaking a cigarette with Armin once
in a while, still wearing short pants and scratchy
woolen kneesocks!

Daniel knew that boy was he, but couldn't con-
nect with him. Some things from back then still felt so
real, he could almost grasp them in his hands. But in
truth nothing from those times remained. . . . And he
wondered out loud, "How can it be that time goes
flashing by and the past disappears just like that?"

"You'd have to get philosophical to answer that,"
Miriam replied.

They'd left Övelgönne behind and tramped on along the sandy gray Elbstrand.

"Time just passes. It slips away. That's what it does," Miriam said. "That's what makes it time."

They were hunched forward a little, hands in their coat pockets. It was a typically grimy, drizzly Hamburg day.

"But that doesn't answer my question," Daniel said.

"True. All right, I'll tell you something Dr. Weizmann said: There really is no such thing as time. There is only one's own life span."

Dr. Weizmann, Daniel knew, was her Hebrew teacher. He had been a philosophy professor. But then the universities had fired all Jews on their faculties. So now he taught languages to earn his living.

"What does that mean, there's only one's own life span?" Daniel asked.

"Here's how Weizmann explained it: The only time span that feels real to you is how long you personally have to live. You look back at how long you've already lived and forward to how long you still have left. That's how you form your perception of time. I'll give you an example: Say you're a creature who lives for three thousand years. So then the time between sunrise and sunset is quite different than if you were a creature with only one week to live. . . ."

That started Daniel thinking, *One week! What if I had only one week to live?*

"Listen, your mother wanted me to talk to you."

"She did? What about?" he asked.

"Well, she thinks you're more likely to listen to me than to her. I'm not sure about that, but, anyway . . ." Miriam paused to watch a tugboat pulling a big freighter upstream. The freighter was from Costa Rica. There were sailors in blue overalls on deck.

"You can probably guess what it's about," she said.

"'The Loreley'?" Daniel had wondered if Dr. Kammacher had called his parents about that.

"Yes, 'The Loreley.' Daniel, you really should be more careful. You only have one more year of *Gymnasium*. You want to pass the senior exams and graduate, don't you? So, don't you think you ought to at least *try* not to get yourself thrown out?"

He shook his head.

A week ago Herr Direktor Doktor Kammacher had read aloud "Die Loreley" by Heine. And afterward he'd confided, "We're really not permitted to study Heine anymore. But this poem is so lovely, and so purely German, I do want us to spend some time on it."

That's so typical of him, Daniel thought. Kammacher prided himself on being broad-minded, liberal about culture, but hard-headed about political matters. He could praise a Jewish poet in one breath and in the next breath compliment the Italian Fascists on their brutal tactics fighting Communists.

"Miriam, do you want to know exactly what I said to Kammacher?" Daniel asked.

"Yes, tell me."

"I said, 'If the Nazis burn Heine's books because he was Jewish, then they shouldn't recite or sing his "Loreley" anymore.' That's all."

"But, Daniel, it's 1937, and we're in Germany!"

Daniel dug his hands deeper into his pockets and gazed down at the dirty sand. "I just think they should be consistent. If they don't want the Jews anymore, then they shouldn't recite poems or sing songs with words by Jewish poets. Also, they should give back to the International Olympics Committee the medals Jewish athletes won for Germany."

She smiled. "Since when have you been thinking things like that?"

"I don't know. I just do."

"Well, good luck." She watched the freighter going by and said, "You know why you're the only non-Aryan still in the *Gymnasium*, don't you?" she asked.

"Yes. Because Kammacher was a war comrade of my father's."

"Exactly. And certain teachers must want you out, because they want their precious Christianeum one hundred percent 'cleansed' of Jews."

"That's so." Teachers like the Ape, for one, who made no bones about it.

"I know I sound like my own grandmother," Miriam said, "but listen, Daniel. Some situations in life demand that you adjust, or else. I had a hard time learning that. You have to learn it too."

She sometimes looked so searchingly at her cousin that he felt she could see right through him.

"And sometimes people our age think we're invulnerable and want to take the whole world on."

"I don't want to take on anybody," he said. "All I want is not to have to hide again. I've done that. All that time I was frightened they'd find me out. And then they did. So at last I can be my real self. I know the truth may get me thrown out of school. But I'd prefer that to hiding."

"I hope you know what you're doing," Miriam said.

They kept on walking. The endless drizzle let up a little, but the wind blew harder. When they got to Teufelsbrück, they sat on a bench and watched a few people hurrying by.

"Sometimes I ask myself what I have to do with them, with those people," Daniel said.

"What do you mean?" Miriam asked.

"They're Germans," he said.

"You're a German too."

"No," Daniel said. "I don't believe I am."

"Why not?"

"I made up my mind about that."

The sky was a chill dark gray now. Only in the far west, where horizon and water touched, could one see a streak of grimy orange-tinted light.

"But if I'm not a German, what am I? I'm not a Jew, either. At most I'm half of one."

"With Jews, there's no such thing. Just whole ones," Miriam answered. "Everyone who has a Jewish mother is a Jew, not half of one."

"Who says?"

"It's written somewhere. In the Torah, I think."

Daniel shook his head. "It's not true of me. I never had any connection with Jewishness, not with the religion nor the culture. I don't feel like a Jew. I never wanted to have anything to do with Jews."

"Why?"

"That's just how it was."

"But you could become one," she said.

"And move to a Zionist training camp?"

"You don't have to become a Zionist right away."

"You've got it easier," Daniel said. "You're all the way Jewish. I'm nothing half and nothing whole."

"Rubbish," she said. "Until '33, I was just as much a German as you. I never knew I was different from everybody else. And I'm not."

"It can drive you crazy," he said.

"Right. And that's why you have to be clear about

213

what side you're on. . . . All right, I'd rather belong to the good side. And that's the Jews."

They both had to laugh.

"But, really," she said. "I'd rather be Jewish than chase after Germans and say, 'Oh, won't you please like me and be nice to me again?'"

"You can't accuse me of doing that," said Daniel.

"No. But you're also not deciding to be a Jew."

Daniel took a while to answer. "Maybe you're right. Maybe it's not the worst thing to be Jewish."

"Ultimately, it's all the same," she said. "Of course, the Nazis don't think so. But they're half-wits. They don't understand. What's important isn't whether you call yourself a German or a Jew. What counts is what you *are*, what you *feel*."

Daniel looked at her, how the tip of her nose moved a little when she talked.

"I think I absolutely don't know what I am," he said.

"And I think you're not the only one."

"But other people always seem to know exactly."

"They just act as though they do," Miriam said.

SOAKING WET

MIRIAM HAD ALREADY FILLED UP THE suitcase she'd arrived with, along with two big crates of things she'd acquired, and she wasn't nearly done.

Tomorrow morning at seven someone from Chevrah would pick her up in the camp bus and drive her to Rissen.

She studied the row of light blue buttons on her night table and couldn't decide: Should she bring them? Would she be needing things like that?

Outside the rain had let up, but she could still hear heavy raindrops falling from the trees. It was almost eight o'clock. She wondered, was Armin still waiting?

The clothes strewn on the bed, the books on the windowsill, and those stupid buttons nagged her. *Finish packing,* she scolded herself. *Get it done!*

She turned, grabbed her raincoat, and came within a hair's breadth of leaving, going *there.* . . . She *had* to see Armin one more time! She knew the friendship between them had to stop. All right, it would stop, once she lived in Rissen.

But now she imagined him at their meeting place, waiting, his shaggy hair soaking wet from all this rain. . . .

It's like with Romeo and Juliet, she thought, *except more so.* The Jewess and the HJ boy. No, worse, the HJ troop leader, because he'd been promoted. And even if he wasn't a real Nazi, the thing between them would end badly. Even though he was so very, very nice. . . .

She checked the clock: a quarter past eight. Now, surely, he wasn't waiting anymore. Nobody waited two whole hours.

Why did I even make this date? she asked herself, although she knew the answer: *I needed to. I couldn't not.* . . .

She thought back to their first walk together in the Elbpark . . . to when he'd put his arm around her shoulders. That felt so good, she'd almost run away.

No one else was there that day, no one watching them. Just squirrels and sparrows. And they weren't interested.

Leaves had rustled underneath their feet. His hand slid over her arm and wandered up; his fingers touched her earlobe. No one had ever touched her like that. The effect was phenomenal. From her skin into her bloodstream. All the way to her knees.

Then they stopped walking. He laid the palm of his hand on her cheek and gently moved her face so that their eyes met. She closed hers. His lips touched her skin. Inside herself she felt both raw and very tender. And then she felt how carefully he pressed his mouth on hers. They both were too excited to open their lips.

They walked on, then stopped again and kissed. And walked some more, then stopped again. And the sun shone through the leaves.

She remembered his body. It felt so good, so slim and muscular. *I have to forget all this, and fast,* she told herself.

A Jewess with an Aryan—"racial desecration," the Nazis called it and considered it a crime. She'd land in a concentration camp. And he?

She went to the mirror on the wardrobe door. She scrutinized her face and told herself once more, severely, *Forget this whole thing, please, immediately. Agreed?*

Agreed, said her mirror self, but not convincingly.

She tried the look that Dr. Weizmann gave her when she'd mixed up articles in Hebrew. She thought of lying down on the bed and dreaming up an ideal prince, one she might meet in Palestine. . . .

Her mirror face frowned and asked, *What about packing?*

She thought, *I'll wake up extra early; I'll finish packing then.*

She brushed her teeth, got undressed, turned off

the light, lay down. She pulled the blanket up to her chin. Out the window, a flock of clouds looking like sheep drifted by; they blanked out the moon.

She pictured those clouds drifting farther on, to other lands. *How long would it take a cloud to make it across the sea,* she wondered, *and then around the whole, whole world . . . while I'm imprisoned here in Germany?*

Something made a scratching sound. She started, thought she saw somebody out her window, and remembered that she hadn't fastened it shut.

"Who's there?"

Slowly, the window swung open. Someone she almost didn't recognize looked in.

"It's me," Armin whispered, and struck a match, so then she could see his face. He was soaked through and shivering.

"How did you climb up here?" she asked.

"It was easy." He blew out the match, slipped in through the window, closed it, and stayed crouching on the windowsill. "Why didn't you come?"

"You scared me! What were you thinking of, climbing in like that?"

"I was worried. I thought something had happened to you. I waited two hours!"

She leaned against the wall and pulled the blanket around herself.

"I waited too," she said.

"But not in the place we arranged!"

"No, I waited here."

"What do you mean?"

"I waited for it to be over."

"For what to be over?"

She hadn't felt tears coming on, but suddenly she was crying. Armin slid down off the windowsill, sat on the edge of the bed, and leaned toward her.

"What happened? Tell me."

"Nothing happened. This has to stop. Armin, we must . . . If anyone had seen us . . ." She burrowed under her pillow for a handkerchief and blew her nose. "If anyone saw you now . . ."

"No one saw me."

"Aunt Sophie and Uncle Rheinhard would go to prison."

"I'm sure nobody saw me," he said.

They heard footsteps on the stairs.

"Someone's coming!"

In a second whoever it was would knock on the door. She pointed Armin to the wardrobe. He tiptoed to it, ducked in, and pulled the door shut.

The footsteps had stopped. A door closed— Daniel's. That's who it was, going into his room.

Armin opened the wardrobe.

"You have to leave," Miriam whispered. "Right now."

He came back to her. "Listen. I waited for hours.

I got wet as a poodle. I worried. Tell me why you didn't come."

"Because," she took a deep breath, "because I'm on the brink of falling in love."

"With me?"

"Exactly. With you."

Armin stammered, "But I—I, too . . ."

"It's better we end it," she said, "and never see each other again. Before it's too late. If we really fall in love with each other, then it'll be much harder to stop."

"For me it's already too late," he said.

Miriam stood, took the blanket, and wrapped it around his shoulders. He pulled it tightly about himself. "I mean it," he said. "I know you are a Jewess and I'm German. But I'm serious—"

"If you are really serious," Miriam broke in, "and if you really love me, then you'll leave now. Because I couldn't stand it. It's already hard enough."

He rose. "And what about if I can't stand it? If I can't bear not seeing you?"

"Then I can't help you. It's not my fault that things are as they are here in Germany."

"You think it's mine?"

"I didn't say that."

"You think it's only unbearable for you? It's bad for us Germans, too."

"That may be," Miriam said. "Let's not quarrel

about who has it worse, Jews or Aryans who go along with all the garbage."

They were silent.

Armin said, "If I go now, I won't come back."

She nodded.

"May I kiss you? Just one last time?"

She nodded again. He moved toward her. He bent forward. Their lips touched.

After a while they drew apart.

They stood in the darkness trying to look past each other. Armin pressed his hands together and said, "Miriam, I know a place where we could meet. Where no one would find us."

"Where would that be? In heaven?"

"No. In my uncle's apartment."

"Your uncle's apartment?" She sounded doubtful.

"He's not there from Mondays to Fridays. He works on a wharf in Rostock; he's a dockworker and comes home only on weekends. Sometimes not even then. I have the key. Because I water his plants and empty his mailbox, things like that."

"And if your uncle comes home by surprise?"

"It wouldn't matter. He's not like that. He wouldn't mind. 'If you have a girlfriend,' he said . . ."

"And how would I get there without being seen?"

"That's what's so great. There's a tailor shop on the ground floor. People are always going in and out. You'd be totally inconspicuous walking past there to the apartment. It's right next door."

They sat again, close against each other. Miriam listened to his breathing, in and out, as evenly as waves on a beach.

The idea was intriguing.

"I just want us to be together," Armin said.

"And no one could spy on us?" she asked.

"My uncle Herbert always leaves the shutters closed." Armin took her hand. "At least come and see it. Will you?"

She pointed to the packing crates. "I'm moving to Rissen, to Chevrah—"

"That's not so far. You could still come. Say you will."

She touched his cheek. "I'll try."

FROM THE ALTONA BALKON, I DROVE STRAIGHT ON, with no goal in mind. After a mile or two I pulled the jeep to the side of the street, leaned back, and closed my eyes.

Only when I opened them again did I realize where I'd driven to. My jeep was parked in front of what looked like a small villa built in the classical style— that is to say, a gracious one-family house of two stories. On the upper story, behind the window at the left, was what had been my room.

Beside the veranda was the little alcove my parents called the winter garden. In front of it bloomed the hydrangea bushes my mother had tended so faithfully.

I wondered who lived there now. The place looked as though it might be empty.

We'd moved out in the winter of 1938 because my father no longer earned enough to pay the rent.

* * *

I grasped the ignition key but did not start the motor. I leaned back and closed my eyes again, felt the sun warm against my skin.

After he'd been thrown out of his office, my father had tried to build up a new practice. One that dealt only with minor matters, nothing in any way political that might come to the Nazis' attention. He invested all his savings in this venture.

My mother would rather have used the money to emigrate. But my father wanted to prove to the world that he could get back on his feet. "Quality always prevails" was his motto.

But it went badly right from the start. My parents had to sell some of their valuable silverware to get by.

Then a letter came from the Ministry of Justice asking my father to declare, of his own free will, that he could no longer act in any legal capacity, not even as a notary public. There was no lawful basis for such a declaration. That was why the letter stipulated that it be "of his own free will." But what did that mean? How could he refuse?

This was blackmail. If he refused, he'd be subject to further harassment. Or be arrested. He had no other choice than to close down his office. For weeks he seemed almost paralyzed.

Trying to find other work was shameful and futile, he thought. He, one of the best-known, most experienced jurists in this city, was suddenly not wanted anywhere.

Finally he took a job as a salesman, selling cattle feed to Holstein farmers. But he did not earn enough commission to afford the rent in the Flottbeker Chaussee. And we moved into a cramped three-room apartment on one of the narrow side streets behind the Altona *S-Bahn* station.

I felt a powerful urge to get out of the jeep, go to the door of the house, and simply ring the bell. But what then? What if somebody opened and asked me to come in? And what if I entered that always-so-dusky foyer and it looked all different now?

It was almost six o'clock, but the sun still stood quite high. Hamburg days are long in June, before the solstice.

How often, I thought, had I run up and down this street? To school and home again, to soccer practice, to the *S-Bahn* station, to Armin's . . . Five, ten thousand times? I shut my eyes and tried to see myself proudly wearing the Christianeum cap on my first day at the new school. My parents had come with me that morning,

225

across the Klopstockstrasse, past the great, dark Christianskirche, past the white town hall, down the Königstrasse to the Hoheschulstrasse. In back of the town hall we'd passed by a little park, kept locked. I found out later that it was the Jewish cemetery of Altona.

On that first day I met Armin. We shared a bench in the third row and didn't exchange a word. I remember staring at his hands. I'd never seen such callused, scratched-up hands. One of his fingernails was all black from some injury. And scrapes and scratches on his arms and shins made me think his life had been more adventurous than mine would ever be.

The next day I convinced my parents I could find my own way to and back from school, and I walked it for all those years.

I sat up at last, started the motor, and made a U-turn.

Then I drove, slowly, at pedestrian pace, across the Klopstockstrasse and the Königstrasse, past where the church and town hall had stood, past what had been the Jewish cemetery—my old, daily route for all those years. Finally I stood again in front of the expanse of rubble that once was Old Altona.

It was on a Saturday in March 1938 that I walked that way to school for the last time.

ASSEMBLY

ON SATURDAY MORNINGS, BEFORE INSTRUCTION began, the whole student body had to gather in the schoolyard: the highest class all the way at the right, the lowest far down on the left. This was the tradition.

Homeroom teachers made certain everyone stood at strict attention.

On the stroke of eight o'clock Herr Direktor Kammacher would emerge from the great portal atop the broad front stairs. He'd cast a sweeping glance over the assemblage, extend his right arm, and salute, exclaiming, "Our Führer, *Sieg Heil!*"

But on the morning of March 12 something unheard of occurred: The students all stood at attention, and on the stroke of eight o'clock, no Dr. Kammacher!

Instead, the assistant director, Knoppe—yes, the Ape!—appeared on the stairs in full SA regalia, desperately trying to stand tall.

Excited whispers circulated. What did it mean? Where was the director?

It was no secret that a power struggle had been

going on. The Ape was ambitious. He'd been longing to topple Kammacher. Had he succeeded? Had he won? But Dr. Kammacher was still the director yesterday! How could such a far-reaching decision have been carried out overnight?

But look, Kammacher was coming after all—not through the portal, but through a side entrance, where he stood with eyes cast down.

The Ape motioned for silence. He skipped the customary roll call—unheard of! He had a matter of immense importance to impart:

"This day will live forever in the history of the Reich. Since early morning, our troops have been marching into Austria. . . ."

Everyone stood still as mice, bowled over by this news. What did it mean? Would there be war? *Yes, war,* was Daniel's first thought. It had been threatening for months, and now it would break loose.

"Our troops have met with no resistance," the Ape continued. "Quite the contrary, they've been welcomed heartily and hailed as liberators. Austria, from now on to be called the Ostmark, becomes a part of Germany, and rightly so! The Ostmark returning home fulfills the dream of 'Greater Germany' that patriots have prophesied since 1848!" Jubilant, almost in tears, the Ape predicted, "Mark my words, thanks to our Führer's courage and resolve, the Ostmark, too, will soon be freed from domination by the Jews!"

Finally he stuck out his chest, thrust his arm forward, and bellowed, *"Sieg Heil!"*

"Sieg Heil!" roared the assemblage (including Dr. Kammacher) as though with a single voice, then again, and many times again, like a phonograph needle caught in a single groove.

Daniel was spared having to salute and shout. "Coming from your lips, *'Heil Hitler'* is an insult to the Führer," the Ape had told him some time before. "You'd best just stand there and keep still."

When the *Sieg Heil* shouting died down, the Ape stepped forward and turned smartly to the right, toward the flagpole, maintaining his stiff military posture as best he could while the gym teacher raised the swastika flag.

The assemblage joined in singing the national anthem: *"Deutschland, Deutschland, über alles / Über alles auf der Welt,"* just one stanza; then the Horst Wessel song: "Raise high the flag, close tight the ranks / SA, march on, with firm and steadfast tread. . . ." These two had long since been conflated into a single hymn.

Daniel looked around.

On other Saturday mornings many boys barely concealed the wry expressions on their faces and shouting *Heil Hitler*, raising their right arms while inwardly intoning, *That's how high the shit is rising—* a witticism that had become a favorite in the school.

Many teachers had mixed feelings too. The music teacher, for one, had shared a secret about the Horst Wessel song with Daniel's class: that the melody was stolen from "Voyage to Africa," a once popular folk song. In any case, on ordinary assembly mornings only a few "150 percenters" stood at rigid attention while it was being sung.

This time, however, everyone sang loudly, wholeheartedly—even Dr. Schnurrbacher, who usually held his arm slackly and hardly moved his lips.

Daniel remembered how thrilled he'd been by the Nazis back in 1933. And even now, though he stayed silent, he wasn't unmoved by the euphoria of this occasion and had to hold himself back from raising his arm and singing along.

Right next to him stood Armin, singing in his deep, growling bass, so wildly off-key, it made Daniel want to laugh—for which he was thankful, because his friend's tunelessness loosened the powerful hold these songs still had on him.

He poked Armin in the side. But Armin was oblivious, his eyes closed, and sang on.

In the past year Armin's looks had changed a lot. His neck was thick now, his shoulders were broad; you could tell by how stocky and strong he'd grown that he was a dockworker's son.

And we're still best friends, Daniel thought wonderingly. At least Armin still acted as friendly as ever. Daniel went to his house twice or even three times a week, and they listened as raptly as ever to jazz. Yet Daniel sometimes felt Armin's mind was on other things, that he acted not so carefree and spontaneous anymore.

"It feels as though you . . . you . . . ," Daniel started to say one time.

"As though I what?"

"You're distancing yourself," Daniel said awkwardly.

"Rot. *Quatsch*," Armin said.

"No, something's not right," Daniel insisted.

Then Armin admitted that yes, he was distracted, and he hinted at a complicated story about a girl.

So that's it, Daniel had thought. But why was he keeping it a secret, when usually they told each other everything?

He felt afraid all of a sudden. What if Armin dropped him? Then he wouldn't have a single friend. He was a stranger among these hundreds of students, all singing and shouting their hearts out. What did he have in common with them? Why was he even standing here?

He turned toward Armin again.

Armin had stubble under his chin, as if he'd shaved in a hurry. He took no notice of Daniel and bellowed with the rest of them, *"Sieg Heil! Sieg Heil! Ein Volk, ein Reich, ein Führer!"*

When the yelling stopped, the Ape moved back a few paces and graciously made room for Dr. Kammacher, who now mounted the stairs, turned to

234

the students, gave one more *"Heil Hitler!"*, and called out, "Dismissed!"

At this moment it became clear to Daniel what had happened: The Ape's "old warrior" status gave him extra prestige. And Dr. Kammacher's job was on the line. So Kammacher had to let the Ape lead this victory celebration. Worse, Daniel sensed that from now on, unofficially but in effect, the Ape would be the leader of the school.

This fear was confirmed when, during second recess, Daniel was called to Dr. Kammacher's office.

Kammacher paced up and down and didn't look Daniel in the eyes. Daniel had always respected the man. But now he only pitied him.

"Affair Daniel Kraushaar," Dr. Kammacher said, trying to smile, and opened Daniel's file. "What am I to do?" He did not expect an answer. "I want very much to keep you on at this school. As you know, your father and I were together at the western front, at the Somme."

"Yes, Herr Doktor Kammacher," Daniel said, thinking that when the director had slunk into the schoolyard, he looked like a soldier ducking, trying not to get shot.

"Daniel, you don't make life easy for me." Kammacher pulled a letter from the folder. "First, the to-do about 'Die Loreley.' And now this business with Winter Aid."

Oh, that. Daniel held back a scornful smile. A few weeks ago the Ape had gotten the idea that the class should take up a collection for Winter Aid—with the dreaded senior exams just months away! That kind of collection would take a lot of time, just when everybody desperately needed every spare minute to cram! The whole class groaned. But only Daniel refused to go along.

"Winter Aid money is spent on rearming," he had said out loud. "Everybody knows it too. People say, 'Look, there goes the Winter Aid,' when Luftwaffe planes fly overhead. And the Party keeps records of who gives how much and gets after people who don't give enough—"

"Quiet, Kraushaar! Sit down!" the Ape had yelled. And then he'd written to the director.

Dr. Kammacher let the letter drop. "Daniel, in your circumstances—you know what I mean— you can't afford to criticize the regime."

Daniel stayed silent.

Dr. Kammacher sighed. "If I tell you something in strictest confidence, will you promise to tell no one—except, of course, your parents?"

Daniel nodded. "Yes."

"You're a—how shall I put it? A thorn in several teachers' sides. Your presence disturbs their instruction." He took another sheet of paper from the folder and read:

"'Having a non-Aryan in the class goes counter to

our nation's most fundamental principle and stance. Even if said student restrains himself from speaking, his very presence is a hindrance to achieving the proper frame of mind. . . .'" Kammacher dropped the sheet of paper. "Do you understand?"

"Yes."

"Even if you *don't* make critical remarks, it's hard enough to keep you in this school."

That's your *problem,* Daniel thought.

The director looked at him for a long while. "What should I do?" he asked.

"I can't tell you," Daniel said.

Dr. Kammacher stood up abruptly. "You leave me no choice," he said, and handed Daniel a letter addressed to his parents.

On the way home Daniel opened the envelope and read it.

Dr. Kammacher informed Herr and Frau Kraushaar "with deep regret" that as of next week Daniel was expelled.

Rheinhard wanted to protest. But Daniel said, "Not necessary." The following Monday he took the S-train to the Dammtor, went into the Talmud-Torah school, the Jewish *Gymnasium,* asked to join its senior class, and soon was enrolled as a student there.

OCTOBER

RHEINHARD DROPPED THE LETTER FROM the Finance Ministry on his desk and carefully smoothed it flat.

"More blackmail," he muttered. The letter requested that he contribute 20 percent of his paid income tax to Winter Aid. Voluntarily, of course. Just as he'd "voluntarily" renounced his right to function as a lawyer.

And what if he didn't comply?

He took a pencil, jotted down numbers: 20 percent of his income tax would reduce his monthly income to less than four hundred mark—not enough to get by.

Daniel's tuition payment was due! Seven months ago, when his son had transferred to the Jewish *Gymnasium*, who'd have thought that coming up with the money would be a problem? Or that things could go downhill so fast?

These days Rheinhard hated opening the mail— bills and more bills he couldn't pay. The electric company had already sent two warnings. Next time they'd threaten to turn the current off.

Even worse was having to beg bank officials to extend him credit. Naturally, they always asked what realistic prospects he had for bettering his income. None. That's what made it so humiliating.

A year ago he was still a successful, respected attorney-at-law. Then Karl had thrown him out as though he were a common peddler. And Rheinhard had thought that was the lowest point he could sink to! That things could not get worse!

They'd have to sell something more, he knew. No matter how much Sophie minded. The piano? Why keep it? It was useless. Every time he or Sophie started to play, the neighbors above and below objected by banging on the ceiling and the floor. Or should he sell the coronation chandelier? It was a wedding gift from Sophie's parents. Or the oak armoire, or the buffet that stuck out and blocked the apartment door?

He glanced around the dingy room with its peeling paint and narrow slits for windows. In addition to the piano, armoire, and buffet, it contained their Biedermeier sofa, two big armchairs, end tables, newspaper racks, two floor lamps, and, squeezed into a corner, Rheinhard's desk and chair. Suddenly it looked to him like a furniture warehouse.

Impossible to keep it in order, in spite of

Sophie's constant dusting and polishing.

Rheinhard's desk, however, was as meticulously neat as ever: the box with writing implements in front; personal-letter file on the right; business-affairs file (including a thick red folder of unpaid bills) on the left.

Rheinhard breathed out heavily. He felt suffocated by so much pressure. This month was almost over, and he had no idea how he'd pay next month's rent. He couldn't think clearly. If he didn't come up with the rent . . . If they couldn't find an even cheaper place . . . Where could they go? Into a homeless shelter? But homeless shelters took in only Aryans. . . .

I should have accepted Karl's offer, Rheinhard thought, *taken that job in his brother's business. But I was too proud.*

The law, jurisprudence, had been his life, his world. He hadn't wanted to write letters for a furniture manufacturer, no. He hadn't understood that by refusing, he'd thrown away his last chance to earn a decent living. Instead, he now sold cattle feed. On good days he earned maybe twenty mark. And on bad days . . .

He stood up, paced back and forth. He couldn't put off paying rent. On November 1, Frau Mager, the landlady, would appear at the door with her pencil and rent book, moving her lips while doing the arithmetic. For some inscrutable reason, the total was always more than the set amount of forty-five mark.

Rheinhard's hand touched the brown envelope in

which he collected money for rent. He didn't need to open it. He knew how much was in it: twenty-five mark.

Four more days till Frau Mager knocked. The woman never actually entered the apartment. He had no way of earning twenty mark and more in that little time. Besides, they also had to buy food and order coal for heat, with winter coming on.

Rheinhard pulled a drawer open, the one in which he kept his precious, specially minted coins. He'd been collecting these for years. Well, he could part with them, and that would pay the rent. . . . But then in December, what would he do?

He read the letter from the Finance Ministry again (as though reading it over and over could make a difference!) and stuck it back into the tax-assessment folder.

"Self-discipline," he reminded himself. That had always been a strength of his. *Don't just sit here brooding over all these unpaid bills, do something: Write a job application, hunt through the Pinneberg telephone book for potential customers.*

He rummaged through the business folder. It contained an offer from a wholesaler: a new kind of poultry feed, very reasonably priced because it was mixed with fish meal. Rheinhard knew about this product. On windy days it stank for miles around, and the hens that fed on it laid seaweed-flavored eggs.

He reread the offer. He tried to concentrate on it.

But a small, framed photo caught his eye. It stood beside his box of writing implements. It was their wedding photo. He and Sophie, in the spring of 1919. She was already pregnant, but it didn't show.

Back then we were just as badly off, he thought. *No, actually worse.* They'd lived in one room without running water, and the landlord had come for the rent not once a month, but every Friday. And they hadn't owned any furniture they could have sold as a last resort or any valuable old five-mark coins, and no bank official would have extended them credit.

Back then, for one whole week, they'd lived on only turnips and potatoes. Sophie had spent mornings at neighbors' and acquaintances' homes, doing seamstress work for very little money—as she'd recently begun to do again.

But then they'd looked to the future with great hope. Rheinhard had his law degree, was admitted to the bar. He worked in a small office. They were newlyweds, awaiting their child. Germany had lost a war the year before but had become a democracy, with free elections. Life could only get better.

And now?

Rheinhold thought back to March . . . Hitler grabbing Austria, a flagrant breach of the peace-treaty terms . . . England, France, and the small neighboring countries paralyzed, letting it happen . . . The Führer triumphant, welcomed by no less a figure than the archbishop of Austria, and happy throngs cheering him on . . . Germans glued to the broadcast of Hitler's speech in Vienna. . . . It dazzled them—they dreamed of even greater glories—and Dr. Goebbels's propaganda kept them dreaming on and on. . . .

And then on April 10, the referendum . . . Yea or nay, in favor of or against the Ostmark's annexation to the Reich. An act of providence, the propagandists called it, and warned, "The hand shall wither that writes nay."

Goebbels had ordered a halt to traffic. . . . Rheinhard remembered the two minutes of ghostly quiet in the city, even pedestrians standing still. . . . Then the cacophony of sirens wailing, ship horns blasting, Luftwaffe planes zooming overhead. And in the evening church bells ringing throughout the Reich.

The radio had broadcast the celebration for one whole hour, and if you listened carefully, you could make out the distinctive *bong, bong* of the great bell called the Pummerin in Vienna's famous St. Stephen's Cathedral. . . .

There were torch-lit parades all over Hamburg, shrouding the skyline in red smoke. . . .

Ninety-five percent of the population voted yea. It was a fraud, some people said. Rheinhard disagreed. He thought Hitler, that common rabble-rouser, had won over the German people. His words and acts embodied the German people's will. . . .

Next on the Führer's agenda: the Sudetenland, the rim of Czechoslovakia nearest the German border. All summer long the propagandists urged that it, too, "come home" to the Reich . . . The newspapers ran horror stories about Sudeten-Germans abused by the Czechs . . . France, Great Britain, and Czechoslovakia called up their reserves . . . War was coming, Rheinhard knew it, very soon. . . .

Instead, there was the Munich conference that September. England gave in and handed Hitler the Sudetenland. The Czechs were not consulted. Not one shot was fired, and the German troops marched in.

Look at all we have achieved, Germany proclaimed. *And now let's solve "the Jewish question."*

Weary and blurry-eyed at his desk, Rheinhard wondered, *Is that wholesale merchant's offer worth considering? Ten kilos of feed for forty-five pfennig, hmm.*

The merchant's name was Schatz. *Sounds Jewish,* he thought. *Just like a Jew, selling inferior stuff. No,* Rheinhard caught himself. He'd been raised on such ideas, which Nazi propaganda now put to notorious use. Of course he knew it was vicious nonsense. And he felt ashamed.

He shoved the letter away and stood up. *Yes, we'll sell something,* he decided. *That chandelier, it looks wrong in this room, the ceiling is far too low. . . .* But he dreaded how Sophie would react.

MY HONOR MEANS LOYALTY, II

ARMIN ENTERED THE HJ OFFICE AND SALUTED, *"Heil Hitler,"* but District Leader Blohm did not respond. He slouched in his chair, with his head in his hand, looking pale. He had dark rings under the eyes. Some moments went by before he sat up a bit straighter, ran his hand across his forehead, and in a hoarse voice said, *"Heil Hitler"* back.

Armin stood at attention by the door. Blohm pulled out a file, riffled through it, and took a long time clearing his throat.

"Young man, young man," was all he said, still riffling, then he leaned forward, coughed, and muttered, "This damned flu!"

He looked at Armin with watery eyes. "We're used to trouble from you, but what you've done now . . ." He left the sentence dangling and held up Armin's file.

"Are there complaints about me?" Armin asked.

Blohm squared his shoulders and straightened up. "Don't act so innocent!" he yelled. "You know perfectly well what this is about."

"I'm sorry, b-but—," Armin stammered.

"No evasions!" Blohm leaned back. More coughing. Then he took a sheet of paper from the file and read: "'Conversation with the superintendent of Plankstrasse number fifty, October 1938.' Does that address tell you anything?"

"It's my uncle's apartment," Armin said.

"Yes, and?"

"I sometimes water his plants."

"And? What else?"

"Nothing else."

Blohm read on, "'The subject, a German of Aryan blood, is the tenant's nephew and has a key to the apartment. He has been frequently seen by the superintendent and several tenants entering and leaving the building. The superintendent was informed that the subject would come to empty the mailbox and water the plants. He knew from his own observations that the subject also used the apartment for secret meetings with his girlfriend. The superintendent informed the subject's uncle of this, to no avail.'"

Blohm smirked, reached for his handkerchief, and blew his nose. That took a while. "'Furthermore,'" he resumed, "'the superintendent observed that the girlfriend in question was dark-complexioned and looked distinctly Jewish. He felt it was his duty to report this to the police.

"'Since the apartment is kept dark, no further observations could be made. A neighbor reported occasionally hearing voices in there and was certain that the nephew and girlfriend were engaging in unseemly behavior.'"

Blohm put the paper down and propped his chin in his hand, looking thoughtful.

"You don't believe all that, do you?" said Armin.

Blohm did not stir. "This is a police report," he said quietly. "You were watched. We've known for a long time who that girl is. The cousin of your friend." He narrowed his eyes. "Be glad I'm not ripping the HJ insignia off your shirt and handing you over to the police."

"I've done nothing forbidden," Armin said.

Blohm stood up, walked around the desk to Armin. He smelled sharply of peppermint oil. "Oh no? Getting together with a Jewess like that? What is the matter with you? I don't understand. You want to join the SS, don't you? You're friends with that half-Jewish boy. . . . Well, he's half Aryan, too. . . . There's a difference between such a friendship and committing racial desecration."

"Nothing like that has happened," Armin protested.

"No, naturally not." Blohm laughed quietly. "You just converse. About Greek philosophy, I suppose. . . . Young man, who would believe that? You'll be called to juvenile court. You'll get thrown out of the HJ. Your SS career is dead."

"But—"

"No 'but'! I don't want to hear any 'buts' from you! Is that understood?"

"Yes, sir."

Blohm turned and faced a cabinet. Armin saw that it had a glass front in which the district leader studied his reflection and was now straightening his uniform.

"If I didn't think so highly of you in other ways," Blohm said, "you'd probably be in reform school right now. Oh, well. Let's not paint the devil on the wall. I'll assume the Jewish slut seduced you. And I want to give you an opportunity to work yourself out of this . . . difficulty. Are you willing?"

"Naturally," Armin said.

"Very well. Something's about to break loose in Germany. The Jews are in for a big surprise. Tremendous. Much more effective than that rather lame boycott of their shops. Bigger than anything yet. When it happens, that will be the time to see your little Jewish whore get what she deserves."

Blohm turned around slowly. "If this matter were brought to trial, it would drag on forever," he went on. "She'd emigrate long before a verdict was reached. We'll do better drumming up a few of our people and smoking out that whole Jewish lair."

"You mean . . . ," Armin murmured.

"I mean the half-Jewish bastard, his all-Jewish mother, his Jew-loving father who married her—"

"The Kraushaars? But Daniel is my friend."

"Stop with that," Blohm hissed. "This will be your only chance." He went to the table and held up the police report. "It won't be long. You will hear from me."

BEFORE THE EXPLOSION

STARTING ON JULY 23, 1938, EVERY JEW fifteen and older was ordered to carry a special identification card with a large yellow *J* on it. Daniel, as a half-Jew, would be exempt for the time being. But Sophie had to have a passport photo taken for which her hair was pulled back and her head bent forward, exposing the left ear, because Nazi research had shown that the shape of the left ear was evidence of racial origin.

To underscore the connection between Jewishness and criminality, fingerprints were necessary too. Sophie was made to press her left and right index fingers on an ink pad, then on the identity card.

In August of '38 a law required all Jewish males to take "Israel" as their middle name; all Jewish females, "Sara." And their passports, emigration permits, tax receipts, and other vital documents—all had to be revised accordingly.

*   *   *

In the meantime, the regime planned its next step: to expel the nearly fifty thousand Polish Jews who lived in Germany.

Most of these had come during the World War of 1914–1918. Actually, a lot of them had been coerced into coming because of the labor shortage in Germany at that time. Their children had attended German schools and grown up more fluent in German than in Polish. But they had not renounced their Polish citizenship. They'd kept their Polish passports, which now the Nazis used as a pretext to drive them from their homes.

When the Polish government (it, too, did not like Jews) got wind of this, it promptly revoked the citizenship of all Polish nationals who'd spent more than five years abroad.

So a grotesque contest between the German and the Polish authorities began: The Germans started expelling Polish Jews in mid-October, sooner than planned; and Poland instantly declared their passports invalid, allowing them two weeks in which to obtain special visas from the Polish consulate. With this move, the Poles seemed to have won the contest, because the Germans could not possibly supply the mountains of data needed by so many visa applicants in that short a time.

In response the Nazis resorted to a more sinister measure: On October 27 they herded some seventeen thousand Polish Jews into holding camps, made them sign "voluntary emigration clearances"—and woe to those who failed to "volunteer."

Early next morning, October 28, they loaded these seventeen thousand onto trucks and drove them to local railroad stations, having made sure the streets on the way would be thronged with angry onlookers shouting, "Out with the Jews! To Palestine!"

The Nazis crammed the Jews into trains and transported them almost to the Polish border. There they were searched. They were allowed to have ten mark on them; whoever had more had to hand it over. Then SS men marched them across fields and over fences right to the border, whipping whoever stumbled or fell behind.

The Poles refused to let them in. The Jews were stranded in no-man's-land between the two borders for several days in rain and cold weather, without shelter or nourishment. Finally the German and Polish authorities came to an agreement: Most of the Jews would be let into Poland; the rest were sent back to Germany.

While the German press rejoiced, calling this a great victory, alarming rumors spread in Jewish circles that inmates at Buchenwald, Sachsenhausen, and other concentration camps were being forced to build new barracks in a hurry, for hundreds, maybe thousands of expected new arrivals.

Everyone could sense it—there was going to be a conflagration. All it needed was a spark, which seventeen-year-old Herschel Grynszpan ignited on the seventh of November.

This young man had fled to France in 1936. The rest of his family, parents and siblings, were among the Polish Jews the Germans deported from Hannover and dumped into a Polish border town. His sister wrote Herschel a postcard describing how they huddled together in an ice-cold barrack, starving.

The postcard arrived on November 3.

Grynszpan was living illegally in Paris. He had tried, in vain, to secure a permit to stay. The police were after him. His sister's postcard was devastating; the young man seethed with rage. He felt he had to do something in protest of his family's ordeal. He'd be arrested anyway, so what did he have to lose?

He made a plan.

He bought a revolver.

On November 7 he went to the German embassy on the rue de Lille with the postcard from his sister in his briefcase.

He told the receptionist he wished to speak with an embassy official, it didn't matter who, and that he had an important document to deliver.

He was shown into a waiting room. No one was suspicious; no one asked him for credentials or gave him forms to fill out. Grynszpan waited a few minutes, then was shown into the office of a minor official, Third Secretary Ernst vom Rath.

Vom Rath offered him a chair and asked the reason for his visit.

"Filthy German, I have a 'document' for you," Grynszpan said. "Here it is. I offer it in the name of many thousands of ill-treated Jews." He reached into his inner jacket pocket, took out the revolver, and shot at vom Rath, who managed to knock him down and flee from the room, calling for help.

Moments later the police took Grynszpan to prison.

Vom Rath was rushed to a hospital and underwent emergency surgery. It so happened the Gestapo had been keeping their eye on him because he was openly anti-Nazi and sympathetic toward Jews.

His fate was not known till the afternoon of November 9.

COUNTING THE CRACKS

"I *DON'T* WANT A DIVORCE. I'VE TOLD YOU A million times!" Rheinhard said, and stormed out of the apartment, slamming the door behind him.

Sophie retreated into the kitchen, sniffling but not crying anymore.

Daniel slumped on the shabby sofa in the living room. He heard the radio in the old deaf lady's apartment next door. The news was on, not loud enough to follow. But he could make out names—Grynszpan, vom Rath, Professor Baumgarten, a surgeon. And he could tell from the announcer's tone that something very serious was going on. Then the neighbor must have turned up the volume because the next sentence came through clearly: "Hitler's personal physician, Dr. Karl Brandt, has arrived in Paris."

Earlier that day Daniel had seen huge headlines: PROVOCATION! OUTRAGE! WORLD JEWRY ATTACKS! Just like last year's headlines blaring INTERNATIONAL JEW-ISH CONSPIRACY! and DIABOLICAL PLOT! when a Nazi leader, Gustlof, had been shot. Daniel remembered

Hitler, furious, speaking on the radio, swearing: "At the next such provocation Jews throughout the Reich shall pay. . . ."

He heard his mother clanking dishes in the kitchen and wanted to go in there, talk to her. But he didn't, because when she was upset, she took whatever he said amiss and kept saying that no one understood her, not her own son and not her husband, either.

She had grown increasingly distressed. The evening after she'd gone to the police for her identity card, she'd scrubbed her hands till her knuckles were raw, but the black ink stains on her fingertips just wouldn't come off. And she had cried and cried as though she'd never stop.

Since then she very often broke down, said unreasonable, hurtful things, and would not let Rheinhard or Daniel console her.

Daniel stretched out on the sofa. He counted cracks in the ceiling. He graded various wallpaper sections on how badly they had faded. He was trying to distract himself from brooding about Sophie. But he couldn't clear her accusations from his mind: "Admit it, Rheinhard! You want a divorce! Don't be such a coward, go on, say it!"

"Why in the world would you think that?" his father had asked. "All I said was that I'm not doing much business these days. What does that have to do with wanting a divorce? I *don't*. I've never once considered it."

Daniel wondered, *Is that really true?*

If Rheinhard got divorced, his troubles would be over. A full-blooded Aryan, he could go back to practicing law, be an attorney again. But without him, Sophie would be unprotected, as much at the Nazis' mercy as all other Jews in Germany.

And Daniel thought, *What would happen to me?* He'd have two choices: He could move in with his father; then he'd be treated like a regular Aryan German, could go back to the Christianeum and later join the Wehrmacht. . . . Or, if he lived with his mother, he'd be criminalized like other Jews.

Whatever he decided, he would not go back to the Christianeum. He'd had stomachaches almost daily from having to sit through racial studies as taught by the Ape and from all that standing at attention, listening to everybody shout *"Heil Hitler!"* and so on. No, going to the Jewish school was a big relief.

But why was he questioning his father's sincerity? In truth Daniel could not recall a single time Rheinhard had hinted at the thought of leaving Sophie.

The trouble was, you couldn't ever really know what went on inside of Rheinhard. *Not even I know,* Daniel thought, *and I've lived in his house for my whole life, I see him every day. . . .*

Maybe her husband's inner life was a puzzle to Sophie, too, so that she could not believe him and therefore kept harping on the subject.

"I don't want you to stay with me out of pity," she'd said when they had finished their midday meal.

"That is not the case," Rheinhard answered.

"But I can feel it," she insisted.

"What exactly do you feel?" Rheinhard asked, and pursed his lips.

"That you don't want me anymore!" She raised her voice. "That I'm a burden to you, a millstone around your neck." And, looking at Daniel, "I'm a burden to my son. If Daniel had a German mother . . . Maybe I should emigrate alone . . ." And back to Rheinhard, "If you married a German woman . . ."

"I don't want to!" Rheinhard shouted, and stood up. "Am I talking to the wall? How many times must I say it?"

That was when Sophie had started to sob.

Rheinhard gave a helpless shrug, took his briefcase, and left. By now he would be sitting in the train, on his way to Pinneberg or Elmshorn.

Daniel looked at the lamp that stood beside the sofa. Its fabric shade had turned a dusty gray, and there were fly specks on the seam. *I'll go and do some homework,* he thought. Just then the doorbell rang.

FINAL WARNING

ARMIN WAS IN HJ UNIFORM. DANIEL ALMOST didn't recognize him, so unprepared was he to see him here, in this apartment.

For a moment they stood not saying anything. Then Armin reached toward Daniel. They clapped hands together, hard. That was their long-standing greeting.

"Haven't seen you in a while," Daniel said. "Come in."

He shut the door behind them and led Armin through the narrow entryway. Sophie came out of the kitchen, wiping her hands on her apron. Her face looked tense but not tearstained anymore.

"It's nice to see you again, Armin," she said. "Should I bring you boys something to drink?"

"I can't stay long," Armin said. "I have to talk with Daniel about something."

"Well, I won't disturb you." She turned back to the kitchen.

Daniel and Armin entered the living room. Daniel

sat on the sofa and motioned Armin to a chair. But
Armin stayed standing.

"It's really been a while. And you've been very
busy?" Daniel asked.

"Oh, you know, HJ duty, and then the senior
exams."

"Oh, right, you took them, last June! Is it really
that long since we saw each other?" Daniel tried not
to sound reproachful.

Armin nodded.

Daniel gazed at him standing by the bookcase
and fleetingly thought that the boyish uniform looked
foolish on a nearly grown man.

"How did it go? I mean, the exams," Daniel
asked, to get a conversation started.

"Less than great. You know, I was never much for
math or physics. . . . But I passed."

"Average grade?" asked Daniel.

"Mm-hm. And you?"

"I won't take them until spring," Daniel said. "I was
put back one semester. The curriculum is pretty different."

"Well, sure." Armin sat finally, but just on the
edge of the chair.

He feels so uncomfortable, Daniel thought, and
asked, "Remember when you used to come visit every
other day?"

"I just haven't had time." Armin stood up, went to
the window, looked down at the street. Then, turning

back to Daniel, he said very seriously, "I came to tell you something. Can anyone hear us?"

"No one's home except my mother, and she's not listening, I'm sure."

"Do you have a telephone?"

"Out in the entryway."

Armin nodded, reassured.

"*Heh*, what's all this secrecy?"

Armin took a breath and started: "Something's brewing. Something bad. If vom Rath dies—" He stopped, sat back down on the edge of the chair.

"They'd use that as an excuse to harass the Jews some more?" Daniel asked.

"A lot worse than harass," Armin said. "Listen. It's going to be terrible. You . . . and your cousin—"

"Miriam? She doesn't live here anymore."

Armin bent forward, thinking, muttering, "Yes, I know."

"You know? How come? Armin, could you possibly be a little clearer?"

"I can't explain. . . . Daniel, you cannot imagine what's about to happen. . . . I'm trying to tell you: You have to get away from here!"

"How do you mean, from here?"

"Out of this apartment."

"Why?" Daniel asked. "I'm only half Jewish. Officially, people like me are tolerated. And Miriam's in the Zionist camp, preparing to emigrate. Isn't that

261

what the Nazis want Jews to do? So why would she be in danger more than others?"

Armin moved to the sofa, close to Daniel, beseeching him, "You have got to hide, my friend. You and Miriam, both. That's all I can tell you."

"Hide where?"

"I don't know. Someplace where no one would think you'd be."

"There's no such place," Daniel said. "I think I'm safer staying home. At least people around here know me. And Miriam's safe where she is."

"Go and hide, I tell you. And Miriam also."

"Armin, enough. Stop with these hints. If you know something, tell me. Or leave us in peace."

"I already said too much."

"No, you didn't. Come on . . ."

Armin put his hand on Daniel's shoulder. "I can only—" Again he stopped himself.

"You can only what?"

"Nothing. I have to go now."

"All right, go, if you're in such a hurry."

"Be well. And do what I said. . . . Hide. Disappear. Just for a few days. That's all."

He went to the door, then turned to Daniel one more time. "Do me the favor. You hear?"

Armin left. The door shut behind him.

Daniel had never seen his friend so troubled, acting so strange.

CRISIS: WHAT TO DO?

RIGHT AFTER SCHOOL ON NOVEMBER 9, DANIEL took the S train to Blankenese and, from there, the bus to Rissen to talk to Miriam.

When he got to the camp, he ran into Sebastian, who was also visiting that day. The three of them went for a walk together through the Rissen forest.

"I have something to tell you," Daniel started, but he found it hard to go on, with Sebastian there.

"It's all right, you can talk in front of my father," Miriam said.

"Armin came to see me. . . . He acted strange . . . said something terrible was about to happen."

"Terrible, how?" Miriam asked.

"You know, against Jews. . . . He said that you and I especially had better hide."

"Why you and me more than others?"

"He didn't say. He said he couldn't."

They walked on, silent, thinking.

It was midafternoon, but already getting dark in the forest. Miriam looked at her father, reached for his wrist, and said, "It's a quarter past four. We want to be back in time for afternoon coffee, don't we?"

"Yes, let's not miss coffee," Daniel said.

They headed back to the camp.

"Obviously, this Armin friend of yours knows something," Sebastian said. "But he won't, or can't, say what or when. Maybe all it amounts to is some HJ boys wanting to get back at you for something. Any idea what that might be?"

Daniel shook his head.

Since changing schools, he had lost touch with his former classmates, all but Peter Mehlhorn, with whom he still listened to jazz now and then.

"No, it can't be just some HJ boys," Daniel said.

"But what has Miriam to do with it?" Sebastian asked.

"I don't understand that either," Daniel said.

"Something about this doesn't add up." Sebastian lowered his head, put his index finger on the tip of his nose. "I don't like how it sounds. I wish your friend had told you more."

"Me too." Daniel looked down at the crinkled leaves on the path. They rustled and crackled. Walking through them felt a little like tramping through snow.

"Armin was scared, and that's not like him." Daniel thought out loud: "He's scared for us . . . and maybe for himself."

Miriam swallowed, took a breath. "I have to tell you . . . ," she started. "I . . . well . . . There was something between us, Armin and me—"

Daniel stood still. "Something like what?"

Miriam and Sebastian stopped too.

"We were meeting each other," Miriam said.

"Where?" Daniel asked.

"That doesn't matter now. In parks. In a café."

Sebastian was appalled. "What did you just say? Meeting an Aryan boy? In a café?"

"Only twice."

"You and Armin?" Daniel stammered. "How come?"

"Just because," Miriam said. "Because . . . I liked him. Such things happen. Or haven't you heard?"

"Well, of course," Sebastian said, "but . . ."

"He didn't say a word about it," Daniel said.

"That was our agreement, not to talk about it with anyone," Miriam said. "Really, no one. Not even one's best friend."

Sebastian nodded. "Of course not. Even so, such a thing can't be kept secret. Half the population are snitches. You know that."

Slowly, they walked on.

"It wasn't my idea," Miriam said. "But he was so persistent. I kept saying we shouldn't. But he just wouldn't give up. And finally we stopped meeting in public places."

"Then where did you meet?" Sebastian asked.

"In an apartment," Miriam said.

"In an apartment? Whose?" Daniel felt shaken.

"We d-didn't . . . ," Miriam stuttered. "It isn't . . ."

"It's all right," Sebastian said. "Whose apartment?"

"It belongs to someone who's away."

They had reached the paved road and turned left. A car came toward them, and they squeezed themselves to the side. When the sound of the motor had faded, Daniel still stared up the road. "How could you get yourself into something like that?" he asked.

"It's already over," Miriam said. "Over!"

"All right, all right," Sebastian said soothingly, but he added, "Of course, that would explain it."

"Explain what?" Daniel asked.

"That warning." Sebastian turned to Miriam. "If there was something between you and that boy Armin, and the SS got wind of it, then we have reason to expect the worst. You're in danger. You too, Daniel, for being Armin's friend. So we'd better decide what to do." He put his arm around his daughter. "Obviously, Miriam, you can't stay here. A Zionist training camp is the least safe place. The safest thing would be if you could hide out with some Aryans."

"Maybe with Frau Paulmann?" Miriam said. Frau Paulmann had been the Kraushaars' neighbor in the Flottbeker Chaussee. "She didn't like how the Nazis

266

treat Jews and made no secret of it."

"That's exactly why you wouldn't be safe with her," Sebastian said. "I think we have to ask Rheinhard to persuade one of his former colleagues to take you and Daniel in for a few days. Come. The sooner we get back to the Kraushaars' the better."

They stopped at the camp, not for afternoon coffee, just long enough for Miriam to pack a few things. Then they hurried to the station and caught the first train back to Hamburg.

THE NOTORIOUS NINTH OF NOVEMBER

ARMIN WAS PICKED TO BE FLAG BEARER of the local HJ group—proof that Blohm had kept his promise not to tell anyone about the relationship with Miriam.

The group stood in formation before the horse-and-rider statue in front of the Altona town hall. Next to them stood the Jungvolk band and the SA flag bearers.

Fires burning in enormous earthen bowls sent flames into the evening sky. This was a sacred date in Nazi history. Streams of visitors, mostly in uniform, pressed into the brightly lit building.

Toward nine o'clock, to drumrolls, the SA, HJ, and little *Pimpfe* started marching. This was the moment they'd waited for impatiently. They mounted the stairs, marched through the portal, through the spacious entrance hall, and into the grand ballroom.

Dramatic half-light seeped through the glass cupola. Garlands festooned the columns in the corners. At the back of the ballroom's stage hung an enormous red flag with a silver swastika in the center and, under it, these words in bold black letters: YOU HAVE CONQUERED AFTER ALL!

The marchers took their positions in front of this flag. The band stood in the first row and played a largo assai by Haydn. "A spirited, stately prelude," the district group leader had commented at rehearsal that afternoon. It lasted about eight minutes and, on account of less-than-virtuoso instrumentalists, was not exactly a pleasure for the ears.

But no matter. Next, an SA man known for his resounding basso recited the words of the hymn "To the Fallen."

Then SA Commander Armbruster ordered, "Lower the flags!"

Now came Armin's moment. Together with three seasoned SA old-timers, he stepped forward and lowered the tip of his flagpole toward the floor.

In deep, firm tones Armbruster explained the reason this was done: "We hereby pay tribute to the memory of our comrades in battle shot by Communist cowards on Altona's Bloody Sunday."

A solemn stillness set in, broken by a muted drumroll. And now the commander called out in a loud voice the names of those who had died fighting at the Munich Feldherrnhalle and here in Altona, during Hitler's failed attempt to take power on November 9, 1923.

After that everyone sang the Kameraden song: "I

once had a comrade, none better will I find . . ."

When the last tones had faded away, Armin and the SA men raised their flags again and stepped back.

The band played an adagio by Schubert. Then came Dr. Bauer's speech, which Armin had been dreading. Dr. Bauer, the regional director of education, was famous for speaking much too long and going around in circles.

He began with an eloquent depiction of November 9, 1923. Then he backtracked to that date of shame in the year 1918, when Communists, Jews, and other scoundrels thrust daggers into the German army's back—an army never before beaten in battle! These same scoundrels caused the Kaiser's downfall, betrayed the Fatherland, and delivered it into the hands of the foe. Well, the Führer had never made his peace with that turn of events. . . . And this brought Dr. Bauer back to where he'd started—namely, November 1923. And the end of his speech was still nowhere in sight. "The tide has turned," Bauer intoned. "We have witnessed a national revolution, yes; our Führer has created Greater Germany. But it is they, the heroes of November 9, 1923, who cleared the way, and we must not forget them. . . ."

When at last the speech was over, the SA and the HJ divisions sang the anthem, "Germany, Holy Word."

For the finale the Nazi party district group leader for Altona stepped up to the speaker's platform. He, too, paid tribute to the victims of Altona's Bloody Sunday, praising their loyalty to the Führer and to his movement. Then he spoke about vom Rath. Late that afternoon it had been disclosed that vom Rath's condition had worsened. "This Jew's cowardly attack must not go unpunished," the speaker declared. "Just as vom Rath was loyal to the Führer, so shall we be loyal, taking whatever road our Führer bids us."

The assemblage swore allegiance to Hitler and joined together singing *"Deutschland, Deutschland Über Alles"* and the Horst Wessel song. It was almost ten o'clock when this solemn celebration ended.

Armin was standing in the courtyard with friends when Blohm, in SS uniform and black cap with silver death's-heads, approached and invited him to the Café Hirt, a favorite watering hole of the SA.

Armin, Blohm, and assorted high officers of the SA and SS crossed the Adolf Hitler Square in front of the Altona railroad station. Armin's friends stayed behind. He felt queasy in his stomach, dreading what might happen, yet at the same time almost burst with pride to be going to the legendary Café Hirt, where HJ boys were not allowed except, of course, in such exalted company.

The place was packed, you could hardly squeeze through, but Blohm cleared a path for them. The atmosphere was raucous. Amidst the jokes and the laughter, though, a rumor circulated. Armin heard it right away—that vom Rath had died of his injuries.

"This could get to be a long night," Blohm said. He sat Armin down at a corner table, ordered him a beer, and told him to wait. Then he went into the club room at the back of the café, where the local leadership was gathered behind closed doors.

Armin glanced around. The noise had quieted. Despite the quantities of beer consumed, the men in here—Armin knew many by sight—looked earnest, determined, had stopped singing and joking around.

"Tonight let's show the world what we're made of!" someone yelled out, and others roared, "We'll drink to that!"

A shiver ran down Armin's back. Brave fighters of the SA had come here long before Hitler's power seizure; it was here they'd gathered courage for their heroic deeds. And now, on this momentous evening, he, Armin Hillmann, sat in this historic place with all these men, all ready for whatever was about to start. . . .

Naturally, neither he nor the others knew just what the officers were planning behind those doors inside the club room. Every once in a while someone came out and spoke into the telephone, which happened to be near enough to Armin so he could make out snatches: "Dr. Goebbels urges everyone . . . resolute . . . relentless . . . In Hesse and Bavaria it has already begun! . . ."

As Armin sat listening and waiting he saw SA troopers from beyond the area come pouring into the café.

Around eleven o'clock the proprietor banged his cane on a table. "Quiet, please! The radio has just announced that our fellow Party member Ernst vom Rath has died of his injuries."

There was a silence. Then the telephone rang. The district group leader was summoned. He spoke briefly, quietly, hung up, turned to the crowd, and said, "Comrades, now it starts."

Men jumped to their feet, formed squads. The district group leader ordered some to go and get gasoline, others to "requisition" cars, the bigger the better, and called for drivers, ones who knew their way around.

Armin was starting to wonder if he'd been forgotten when Blohm and an SA storm trooper came out of the club room straight toward him.

"Do you know what will happen tonight?" Blohm asked.

"An action against the Jews," Armin said.

"Yes, a new sort of action. One unlike anything the Hebrew pack has experienced." Blohm stepped up close to Armin. "Do you know what that means as far as you're concerned?"

Armin shook his head.

"It's your chance to straighten out your situation. Your first and only chance." Blohm shouted at him, "Is that understood?"

"Understood."

WE INTERPRETERS WERE BILLETED AT A SMALL, pleasant hotel on the Alster. The four of us had many comforts there, including our own table in the officers' club.

That evening the air was balmy. We sat on the terrace, where my colleagues began a game of skat. I just watched.

"What's trump?" Hans asked.

"This," said Valentin, and played the nine of diamonds.

Hans came from Baden—you could hear it in his accent. Valentin's was not that easy to trace, but I knew that he was born in Berlin, grew up in Budapest and Mainz, and had emigrated to London with his whole family back in 1933.

Herman, the third player, came from Hamburg, like me. Both he and Hans had left Germany in '33, soon after Hitler's rise to power.

Herman loved skat. He was always ready to play, even though he always lost.

I wasn't keen on it and played only when they couldn't find someone else to be their third. The game held too many memories for me. . . .

We'd played skat during recess, Armin and I, when we could find a third and sometimes during class if we were bored. And when we played at Armin's house, it wasn't so much to win as for the raunchy rhymes Herr Hillmann recited when certain cards were turned up. We memorized a few of those to impress our class-mates when we played skat at school.

Valentin shuffled lightning fast, just like Armin's father. Then he slid the deck over for Hans to cut.

Hans didn't touch it, just rapped his knuckles on the table—as Armin used to do.

Valentin dealt the cards, first three, then two, then four, then three again, and right away my colleagues started teasing: "Eighteen, twenty, two, zero, four . . ."

Every German knows this row of numbers by heart. Armin used to drill me on it: "Eighteen, twenty, two, zero, four, seven . . . You have to know it in your sleep, so you can rattle it off if someone is getting you out of bed in the middle of the night. . . ."

I only pretended to watch the skat game. I was really seeing those children's faces in my mind, the ones

275

who'd gathered around my jeep on the Altona Balkon. They looked about the age I was when Armin taught me the game. I could feel their eyes on me, their total amazement. They couldn't believe it—because I gave them chewing gum!

Not allowed! Unheard of! Because of Supreme Commander Montgomery's "nonfraternization" rules, which forbade Allied troops soldiers waving, or even smiling, if any Germans waved at us; nor were we to play with German children, nor offer them chocolates or gum.

The reasoning behind these rules was that the entire German nation bore the blame for the crimes of the past years and should be treated accordingly.

With a shake of my head, I tried to stop brooding and pay attention to the game.

Hans had a grand slam in his hand and looked to Herman for clues about what to do next, but Herman's expression gave nothing away.

They certainly weren't thinking about Germany's collective guilt right then. It didn't seem to worry them at other times, either. . . .

I hadn't told them about my tour through Altona. And I wasn't going to. Not that I thought they'd report me for breaking the rules. I just figured they wouldn't understand. Because they pretty much acted as though they had no connection with this country anymore. As children, they'd spent a few years here, had learned the language and things like playing skat, and that was all.

I thought perhaps the difference was that they had left so early. People who'd stayed longer, and experienced what life was like under the Nazis, somehow clung to this land much more fiercely. It wasn't clear to me if this was despite, or in some strange way because of, the mortifications and suffering they had endured. . . .

Hans drew a card, laid down another; the game went on. And I went on thinking about what I'd seen and felt that day, driving through the part of the city in which I had grown up.

What took my breath away as much as the total devastation I beheld in Old Altona was that the Flottbeker Chaussee looked exactly as it had on the summer's day six years before when I had seen it last.

Here stood the stately houses with their fancy façades (some of the trim in need of repair, but this had always been so). Here stood the venerable oak and beech and chestnut trees. And the gardens in front were well tended, the hedges neatly clipped. It was uncanny, this little world, so sheltered, unaltered, and unto itself.

The four-story house on the corner bore a faded billboard predating World War I. It made me feel trapped inside an old, deserted movie set. If there'd been people around, the scene would not have seemed so unreal—because war leaves its imprint on people, even if they're well-to-do. But the only person I caught sight of, and only from the rear, was an old woman dressed in black, sweeping the sidewalk in front of her garden gate.

Along this gracious boulevard there was nothing to remind one of the ten thousand Hamburg Jews taken off to extermination camps, the thousands of political dissenters tortured and killed, or the fact that in Neuengamme, quite nearby, countless children were maimed and murdered in "medical experiments."

Here, where everything still looked the same, you could persuade yourself that no atrocities had been committed. There were other such neighborhoods too.

But why was I so surprised? What had I expected? Six years in the lifetime of a city is not long. Why, after all, would things have changed in an area which the bombing raids had spared?

*   *   *

My three colleagues were done playing. Our beer glasses were empty.

Valentin asked, "Shall I get us another round?"

Before we could answer, a British officer came to our table.

"Lieutenant Kraushaar?" He mispronounced it "Kraushoar."

"Yes, sir?"

He informed me in clipped tones that I was to report to Neuengamme in the morning.

The former concentration camp was now a holding place for Wehrmacht soldiers. And Montgomery had ordered their release. There was a shortage of farm-workers, and these soldiers could be used to bring in the harvest. But first they had to fill out forms and be questioned at hearings, for which interpreters were needed.

I asked if I would have to change my living quarters.

The answer was yes.

Hans clapped me on the shoulder. "Too bad, Lieutenant 'Kraushoar.' It won't be as luxurious as here."

"We'll miss you," said Valentin, and went for another round of beer.

WAITING

"IT'S ELEVEN THIRTY ALREADY," SOPHIE SAID. "Rheinhard said he'd be back in just a little."

"He'll be back," Sebastian said.

Herr Kraushaar had gone to ask a former colleague to take Daniel and Miriam in for the night. It was nearly ten o'clock when he'd left the apartment.

Meantime, the radio reported that vom Rath had died.

Sebastian turned the dial. He hoped there'd be a German-language newscast on the BBC. But there was only a concert. He switched the radio off.

Daniel went to the window. It was unusually quiet outside, no one about.

"I heard that nothing much is expected to happen on major streets," Sophie said, "because they don't want the foreign press to find out."

"Everyone has heard something or other," Sebastian said. "It seems that even the Nazis aren't sure exactly what's ahead. Only the Tadpole knows."

"Why do they call Goebbels the Tadpole?" Miriam asked.

She sat in the armchair by the window. Daniel turned to her and answered, not too loud, "Because all a tadpole has is a head and a *Schwanz*."

"Daniel!" Sophie gave him a reproachful look.

Then everyone was quiet.

All of a sudden, a thud. They all started. Daniel swallowed hard. Something in the apartment above them must have dropped or tipped over.

In any case, it had nothing to do with them. Daniel breathed out. He tried to calm himself. His stomachache was back. He'd been free of it for a while, but lately it was sometimes so bad, he needed to lie down.

He looked out the window again. A fine drizzle made the black pavement gleam. Across the street a man who worked the night shift was coming home. He groped in his pockets for his keys. Then he opened the door and went in. *As he does every night,* Daniel thought, and told himself, *Maybe this night will be ordinary, just like any other.*

But he didn't believe it. No, tonight would be different. He could feel it in his body, and the waiting made his chest constrict.

"We're sitting here in a trap," Miriam sighed.

Sophie's eyes were locked on the clock as though staring at it could speed up Rheinhard's return.

283

"They've taken everything away from us," she said. "First our property, then our rights as citizens. What more do they want?"

"To get rid of us," Sebastian answered. "That's what they want."

"Then why do they take people's last pennies when they're trying to leave? They know perfectly well that no country lets in people without money," Sophie said.

Sebastian shrugged his shoulders.

Silence again.

Daniel traced his finger along the cracks in the paint of the window frame. For a second or so he let his forehead rest against the cool glass. Outside the only sound was the wind.

In his mind he kept hearing Armin's warning. His friend had sounded so vague and confusing, but one thing was certain: He hadn't been joking.

Sophie sighed. "Where can Rheinhard be?"

They heard the door, then footsteps through the entrance hall.

Rheinhard came into the living room. He used his handkerchief to dry his hair.

"The streets are full of SA," he said.

"What did your colleague say?" Sophie asked.

"Colleagues, plural. Not much." Rheinhard shook his head. He took off his coat and scarf and hung them in the wardrobe. "I went to see Franke. And

Kleinschmidt. It's tragic what these people have become. They're frightened. They're just hoping to save their own skins."

"And what will happen now?" asked Miriam.

"You have to stay here," Rheinhard said. "Anything else makes no sense. It's getting ominous out there."

"But Armin said we absolutely must not stay here," Daniel said.

"So where can you go?" Rheinhard motioned toward the window. "Whoever ventures out tonight had better be Aryan and wearing a Party badge."

"We can't just sit around here waiting," Daniel argued.

"We can't do anything *but* wait here," Rheinhard said. "Nothing else makes sense."

He sat down at the table and took Sophie's hand.

Miriam started to say, "I think . . . I know a place where—"

But Rheinhard interrupted. "You're anxious, I can understand. That fellow Armin was exaggerating. Possibly he'll turn up here with a few of his HJ friends. But what can they do? We have nothing to hide. And people who're not hiding anything needn't hide themselves. That would only arouse suspicion."

"You don't believe that crap!" Daniel was startled at how loudly he'd spoken.

Sophie said, "Daniel, you mustn't use such language."

A year ago Rheinhard would have slapped him down. But now he did nothing, just sat there looking powerless.

Daniel felt frantic, out of control, fed up with sitting around just waiting, sick of all the awful rumors, and even sicker of his father's lame assurances. "I don't want to hear it anymore!" he burst out. "All that 'reasonable' talk! 'Reasonably' viewed, things in Germany aren't that dramatic. 'Reasonably' understood, we're not so badly off. 'Reasonably' considered, there's no urgent need to emigrate. 'Reasonably' regarded, if you behave properly, stick to the rules . . ."

He confronted his father. "Why did Uncle Karl throw you out of the practice? Surely not because you did anything wrong!"

Rheinhard avoided his gaze. "You don't understand."

Daniel felt unstoppable. "Whatever happens, the main thing is that your desk will stay in perfect order," he shouted. "That is your sad philosophy of life."

"Let's not make each other look bad, my boy."

"But I'd just like to know what you *feel*!"

Sophie stood up. "Daniel, that's enough. Really."

He turned to her and said, "You can't stand it anymore either."

Sophie moved close to him. "Get a hold of yourself, Daniel."

He breathed out noisily.

At last Rheinhard looked him in the eyes and said, "Reason is our highest good. It's important that we hold on to our reason, even when we're facing inhumanity."

No one answered. Everyone looked past everyone else. Daniel turned back to the window.

Just then the window shattered. Shards of glass came flying in; a stone landed on the floor.

"Jews up there!" somebody shouted.

They all stood as if frozen.

"They're coming," Rheinhard said.

You could hear them downstairs, banging on the door. Someone shouted, "Open up!"

Any moment the block warden or somebody would smash the house door in.

"We have to get away!" Daniel grabbed Miriam's hand. "Mother, Father, Sebastian, maybe you should also."

"Where should we hide?" Sophie asked despairingly.

"No need." Rheinhard put his arm around her. "We did nothing wrong. We're staying."

Sebastian kissed Miriam. "Take care of her," he said to Daniel. "Don't worry about us. Go on, climb out the kitchen window, hurry!"

THE HEARING

SOPHIE WATCHED THEM SQUEEZE THROUGH and clamber down the wall. Once on the ground they looked carefully around. No one in sight. They ran through the backyard to the rickety fence, scrambled over it into a parking lot, and disappeared among the cars.

Meanwhile, Sebastian locked the door to the apartment. Jeers and insults came from outside.

Rheinhard stood in the hall and telephoned the police. He reached the precinct, described the situation, was silent a moment, then put the receiver down.

"What did they say?" Sophie asked.

"They just laughed."

He turned quickly around, because whoever stood outside was beating hard on the door, making the doorframe creak. Sophie cried out, terrified. Sebastian started pushing a heavy chest of drawers against the door.

"No." Rheinhard held him back. "We need not barricade ourselves in. We have nothing to hide."

The blows to the door grew stronger. The hinges were cracking apart.

Sebastian's face contorted. "Rheinhard, they'll break the door down!"

Rheinhard said, "They won't do that, because I'll open it. Go in the bedroom and stay there. You too, Sophie. Shut yourselves in."

Sebastian did not budge.

"I'm still someone to be respected," Rheinhard said. "I'm a decorated war hero. In this apartment no danger will threaten you."

He pushed Sophie and Sebastian toward the bedroom. Then he went to the door, unlocked and opened it. Before him stood half a dozen men wearing shabby coats over their SA uniforms.

"What is it you want?" Rheinhard asked.

He got no reply. One man grabbed him by the collar, banged Rheinhard's head against the wall, and shoved him out of the way. Then they all entered the apartment.

They started attacking the furniture. One took a hammer to the lamp in the entrance hall, which crashed down in pieces, almost hitting the man in the face.

The thing that interested them most was the glass-doored breakfront. The good dishes were kept in there. Using sticks and cudgels, the SA men swept the dishes to the floor and trampled them to shards. Then they emptied the bookcase, threw the books out the window onto the street. One man took a bread knife from the kitchen and went around slashing all the paintings.

Rheinhard stood squeezed against the wall in the entryway. All he could do was look on mutely. When he turned, he saw an SS man in black uniform standing in the door. It was Blohm. Next to him stood a boy with a civilian coat over his uniform. Rheinhard didn't recognize him right away. But then he realized it was Armin, best friend of his son.

Blohm grabbed Rheinhard by the shoulders and shoved him into the living room. He turned to the men who just then were smashing the old grandfather clock apart with hammer blows.

"That's enough," he commanded. "That's not what we're here for. We're looking for the whore and the bastard. Hillmann, search the apartment!"

"Yes, sir." Armin walked stiffly, first into the kitchen, then to Daniel's room. The door to the bedroom was locked from inside.

Armin returned and reported, "No one here, although one room is locked."

Rheinhard started to say, "That's where my wife and—"

Blohm slapped him in the face. "No one asked you." He turned to an SA man carrying an axe. "Go take a look."

The man went. One could hear the heavy blows, wood splitting, and Sophie shouting, "Stop! I'll unlock it!"

Seconds later the man pushed Sophie and Sebastian into the living room.

"No one else in there?" barked Blohm.

The SA man shook his head.

"Search the place!" Blohm ordered.

You could hear the men tearing wardrobes open, emptying them, tipping beds over, destroying whatever was in their way. In a few minutes they came back.

"No one else here," they reported.

"Where are they? Where did they hide?" Blohm yelled.

"Whom do you mean?" Rheinhard asked.

Blohm slapped him again. "Don't play stupid. We're looking for your son, the Jew bastard, and the Jewish whore. Where are they?"

"I don't know," said Rheinhard.

"You lie!" Blohm turned to Armin. "You conduct this hearing."

"Yes, sir," Armin said, straightening his posture, standing tall.

The SA men made themselves at home. They sat on the sofa and in the chairs they'd ripped open, lit up cigars they'd found in a drawer, and looked on with interest.

"Hillmann, go ahead, question him," Blohm ordered.

Armin took a step forward. Not looking at

Rheinhard, he said, "Herr Kraushaar, do you know where Daniel and Miriam are?"

Blohm started to laugh, as did the SA men.

"You won't get much out of him that way," one called.

"Boy, you have a lot to learn," another man said jovially. He grabbed a full bottle of cognac out of the sideboard, took a deep swallow, and passed it around.

Blohm laid his hand on Armin's shoulder. "I'll show you how this is done." He stood square in front of Rheinhard and bellowed in his face, "Where are your Jew-bastard son and the Jewish whore? Answer!"

Then he gave Rheinhard a resounding smack and turned to Armin. "That's how. Now you."

"Be brave!" called one of the SA men. "You can do it!"

Armin approached Rheinhard and asked, "Where are your son, the Jewish bastard, and the Jewish whore?"

"Too soft," Blohm yelled. "Louder!"

"Where are your son, the Jewish bastard, and the Jewish whore?" Armin repeated somewhat louder.

Rheinhard looked aghast at him.

"Louder!" Blohm yelled. "And don't forget the smack!"

Armin pulled himself together and screamed, "Where is your son?"

"Go on!" urged Blohm. "Go on!"

Armin couldn't utter another word.

"Get a grip on yourself," Blohm hissed. "If you fail at this . . ." He shoved Armin up against Rheinhard.

"Where are your son, the Jewish bastard, and the Jewish whore?" Armin yelled as loud as he could.

"Now the smack!"

Armin slapped Rheinhard in the face.

"That was nothing," said one of the SA men, dropping cigar ash onto the carpet.

"Harder!" Blohm yelled. "Go on!"

Armin slapped Rheinhard again.

Rheinhard looked at him and said, "Boy, what have you become?"

"Shut up!" Blohm screamed, and gave Rheinhard another smack.

"Stop!" cried Sophie, bursting in.

"Get this whore away from me!" Blohm shouted.

Two SA men sprang up, grabbed Sophie, and dragged her into the next room. Sebastian followed them. A dull blow could be heard, then an SA man's voice: "Make sure she stays here and keeps quiet."

The two men came back.

"I've had enough," said Blohm.

He pulled his revolver from its holster and put it to Rheinhard's temple. "All right, out with it. Where are they?"

"I really do not know," Rheinhard answered.

Blohm cocked the revolver.

"For God's sake," cried Rheinhard, "what wrong have I done?"

Blohm repeated, "Where are they?"

"I don't know. Listen. I am Aryan. I am an attorney-at-law. This outrage will have consequences."

"Don't talk nonsense," Blohm said. "When you're dead, none of that'll do you any good."

Rheinhard had closed his eyes. His entire body trembled. "Listen to me," he moaned. "I was at the western front. I received the Iron Cross."

"Let's see it!" Blohm growled.

Rheinhard hurried to the chest of drawers, extracted the black metal box, plucked up the Iron Cross, and held it out to Blohm.

Blohm looked at it. "Seems genuine," he muttered. He stuck his revolver back in the holster, straightened up, and hit Rheinhard with his fist. Rheinhard staggered backward but stayed on his feet. His lip had burst open and was bleeding.

"You're lucky you were at the front," said Blohm. "If not, you'd be over."

He smoothed his uniform and turned to the SA men. "We're finished here. Let's go. There's still a lot to do tonight." He looked around the wrecked apartment and said, "Goddamned pigsty here." He turned and leaned his arm on Armin's shoulder. "Didn't you say something about a Zionist training camp? I wouldn't mind taking a look at it."

IN HIDING

DANIEL AND MIRIAM HURRIED TO THE
Bahrenfelder Strasse and on from there toward the
Altona train station. Groups of SA and SS stood
around in the Spritzenplatz. Miriam wanted to back-
track and go a different way, but Daniel said, "That
might attract attention. We'll be less conspicuous if
we just walk past them on the sidewalk."

Glass splinters from the two Jewish-owned stores
in the Bismarckstrasse covered the sidewalks and the
street.

When Daniel was little, he'd often stood in front
of the window of the housewares store. He'd loved to
look at the cooking pots stacked to make a tower and
at the preserve jars arranged into a pyramid, topped by
a bright enamel bowl, and at the shiny silverware
lined up in symmetrical rows.

Now the shelves were broken, the jars all
smashed or strewn about, the pots so badly dented,
they'd probably been trampled on. Looters rummaged
around for anything left whole, worth plundering.

No police were anywhere in sight. A few pedestrians going by seemed quite indifferent.

Miriam and Daniel caught the number 27 streetcar to the Sternschanze. The ten-minute ride felt like an eternity. Getting out on the Weidenallee, with its many Jewish-owned stores, they had to tread their way through heaps of broken glass.

They turned into a narrow side street. Miriam stopped in front of a sign reading TAYLOR SHOP A. BRECHT, GROUND FLOOR, LEFT. The door to the house was not locked. Miriam seemed to know her way; she went straight through the building and out the back door, behind which was a flowerpot and, under it, a key.

She came back with the key and opened a door on the ground floor to the right.

"What kind of place is this?" Daniel asked when she had shut the door behind them.

"Armin's uncle's apartment. And he never comes here during the week."

All the shades were drawn; the place was pitch dark. Miriam didn't switch on any light. She struck a match and led Daniel into the living room.

"Sit down someplace." She blew out the match.

They sat across from each other. After a few moments Daniel was able to see the outlines of the furniture.

"His uncle lives here just on weekends?" Daniel asked.

"Yes. He's a dockworker in Rostock and almost never comes home."

"How did you know where the key was?"

"We used to come here. Armin and I."

"Oh . . ."

They sat for a while in the dark, talking in whispers about what they'd seen on the way. Finally they fell asleep, exhausted.

When Daniel woke, he heard noises outside. Miriam crept to the window, raised the shade a little, and peered out. It was early morning. A thin stripe of light fell into the room.

Daniel stretched and came to the window.

"Look back there," Miriam said. "See that kosher butcher shop?"

Yes, Daniel saw. SA men were smashing it up. A few people stood around and watched. They weren't cheering or jeering. Maybe they didn't approve. But nobody protested.

"Behind there, see the smoke? That's from the synagogue," Miriam said. You could hear the fire-engine bell from the Altonerstrasse.

Furnishings from another shop were being hurled into the street. People moved out of the way. Two SA men dragged out the owner. He had a white beard and wore a yarmulke.

They beat him and stomped on him.

"A defenseless old man," Miriam murmured.

"And no one does a thing about it," Daniel said.

The old man lay on the ground, not moving. An SA man pulled him up. Another grabbed the white beard with both hands and yanked on it.

The old man regained consciousness, howling with pain. The SA man kept yanking out beard hairs.

Some people craned their necks to get a better view. Others went their way, shaking their heads. The SA man laughed, pulled and pulled.

"It's not just that it hurts him," Miriam said. "The beard is holy to him, and they know it."

Daniel put on his coat and went to the door. Miriam followed, held on to him. "Stay here! I know exactly how you feel. But it's pointless. You can't do anything out there. You're all alone. You're a half-Jew. They'll stick you into a concentration camp!"

"But one can't just look on," Daniel said. "I don't understand how those people can simply stand there."

"Shh, not so loud," Miriam whispered. "You know the walls have ears."

She pulled him back into the room. It wasn't so dark anymore. Light seeped in through slits in the shades. They sat together on the sofa.

"You think we can stay here awhile?" he asked.

"Yes. The uncle won't be back before Friday."

Daniel leaned back. On the opposite wall hung a kitschy painting of a stag hunt. The furniture looked thrown together. *Typical bachelor's apartment,* he thought. It bothered him that Armin had never told him about this place.

Miriam sat twirling locks of hair around her index finger.

"So you two met each other here?" Daniel asked.

"Yes," she said. "Do you mind?"

He thought it over and answered, "Yes."

"Why?"

"Well, he's my best friend . . . was, anyway. And you're my cousin."

"So?"

"Did you . . . when you were here, did you . . . ?"

"None of your business," Miriam said.

Daniel nodded. "Right."

Miriam rested her head on the arm of the sofa and closed her eyes, then sat straight up again.

"We didn't do it, Daniel," she said. "Actually, we meant to. But . . . well, it didn't happen."

"Why not?"

"Man, you sound like a father confessor."

"Now you clam up, just when it's getting interesting!"

"Yes, because it's private. Anyway, I'm glad we didn't."

"Why?"

"Because . . . just because, that's all."

Daniel looked again at the stag-hunt picture. How

much effort there was in it, how many painstaking brushstrokes! And even so, it was awful. He stood up, went to the window, held the shade up a bit, and peered out.

The street was empty now.

Miriam started. "Daniel!"

"What?"

"In the hall . . ."

The next moment a key turned in the lock. The apartment door opened.

"Someone's here!" Daniel whispered.

"The uncle!"

Miriam looked around the room. Where could they hide? They grabbed their coats, squeezed into the space between the wardrobe and the wall, and held their breaths.

CROUCHED IN THAT SPACE, MIRIAM AND Daniel could see only the boots and coat hem of the man who had entered.

He was breathing hard. He crossed the room. He sank into a chair. There he stayed.

After a while he made an odd sound, a sob. That turned into soft, unmistakable crying. Daniel and Miriam looked at each other, wondering. Carefully, Daniel moved his head forward enough to see past the wardrobe.

He couldn't tell who was slumped in the chair, his head turned to the side. Definitely not the uncle. Because under the shabby coat, now open, he wore the HJ uniform. Not making a sound, Daniel stood up and, recognizing him, crossed the room.

Armin looked up and groaned.

Miriam came to them.

Armin rubbed his hand across his face. "Man, you gave me a scare! How did you get in?"

"I knew where the second key was," Miriam said.

Armin drew in his breath. "Good for you." He started laughing quietly. "So here you both are. . . . And nobody figured it out."

He kept laughing and buried his face in his hands.

"What's wrong with you?" Daniel asked.

"What should be wrong?"

"Why are you laughing?"

"Because it's comical. Comical and tragic. If you knew what I lived through tonight . . ." Armin sat up a little and looked off into space, then at Daniel with empty eyes. "Anyway . . . your parents are all right. Your father was, er, questioned. But he came to no harm. Compared to other people."

"You were at our apartment?" Daniel asked.

Armin nodded.

"With the gang that broke in?"

"He opened up himself, your father. Acting correctly, as always."

"You led them to us?"

"Man, they know where you live. They would have found you anyway."

"And what happened then?"

Armin raised his shoulders. "They didn't find you, or you." He looked at Miriam. "Lucky! Man, they wanted to. They wanted to finish you off."

Daniel sat down on a chair and stared at the rug. "You were in our apartment," he said, shaking his head, "with that whole SA mob."

"How not?" Armin said. "What else could I have done? I didn't want them to find you. I warned you, remember? If it gets out that I did, I'll go straight to Fuhlbüttel or some other concentration camp! Plus, I'll get kicked out of everything. I *had* to lead them to your apartment! So they wouldn't catch on that I warned you. . . . Besides, they made me do it."

"Made you? How?" Daniel asked.

"Man, you have no idea," said Armin. "They put pressure on me. They knew about me and Miriam."

"How could the two of you—?"

"Shh, Daniel." Miriam put her finger to her lips.

Armin stood up. "My career is over," he said. "My whole future, and you know why? Because I didn't betray our friendship."

Daniel leaned back. "You sound as though you've suffered some god-awful tragedy."

Armin faced Daniel. "You don't understand. If I hadn't warned you, we wouldn't be having this conversation, because you'd be sitting in Fuhlbüttel. Instead, you're here, in my uncle's apartment. Which I'm responsible for. So I actually should be going to the police right now. But I'm not. So I'm taking still another risk for you. What else am I supposed to do?"

"I'm not the one to ask," Daniel said.

A CLOSER LOOK

THEY'D WATCHED THE SMOKE RISE LONG enough. "Now let's go see the great synagogue it's coming from," Miriam said.

"Too dangerous," Daniel said. But she insisted.

They went through the Schanzenpark, past the redbrick water tower, past the train station to the Rentzelstrasse. The burning smell grew stronger.

This was the Grindel district. Its many Jewish stores had all been savaged. By now it was broad daylight, but that didn't stop the looters, among them SA men with civilian coats on over their uniforms so they wouldn't be too conspicuous. Others were busy doing their jobs: spitting on the Jewish store owners, beating them up, and hauling them away.

The streetcars were not running, and there was hardly any other traffic, which lent an eerie stillness to the scene.

A piano lay shattered smack in the middle of the Grindelallee. Daniel imagined how much trouble it must have been to heave it through the window, yet the SA had done it, thought it worth their while.

He and Miriam crossed to the Bornplatz and stood before the synagogue. Its noble cupola had fallen in. It wasn't burning anymore, just sending up puffs and wisps of smoke, as though the ruin were breathing. Two thirds of its stone sidewalls still stood, blackened with soot. The stained-glass windows lay in pieces all over the sidewalk.

"I was never inside," Miriam said. "I never believed in the Jewish God. But I wanted to see this."

They were the only ones standing there. Other people rushed past without stopping.

Miriam picked up a bit of sea-green glass. It had a hairline crack down the middle. She gazed at it. Then, gripping it tightly, she snapped it in two, gave one piece to Daniel, and put the other piece in her coat pocket.

"It's to remind us," she said. "For when we tell our grandchildren about this day."

That afternoon, when Daniel and Miriam returned to the Kraushaars' apartment, Sophie and Sebastian were putting things back in order as best they could. Rheinhard lay on the sofa. He had black-and-blue marks all about his face and a bandage over the stitches in his lower lip.

Then Miriam and Daniel heard what had happened in the night, how Rheinhard was "questioned," what role Armin had played.

So that explained the weird way Armin had laughed, how he'd sounded, and the things he'd said, thought Daniel. And he felt something dying—a part of him. He could feel himself letting it die—the friendship that, for so many years, had been about the most important thing in his life.

Sebastian found a German-language broadcast from Denmark on the radio:

Synagogues on fire. Stores demolished throughout all of Germany. Mass arrests. Jewish men aged eighteen to sixty rounded up, forced into trains, taken to concentration camps. "Jewish men, stay indoors," the newscaster urged.

The Kraushaars were growing short of food. Rheinhard still felt too weak to walk.

"I'll go shopping; it's less risky for me," said Daniel with a glance at Miriam. And he went.

While waiting his turn at the corner grocery, he listened to other customers talking. They mentioned some stores they'd heard were broken into and Jews who'd been arrested. No one said a word about anything he or she might personally have done. They sounded disconcerted by the sudden outbreak of the violence. Some hinted that it was senseless, wasteful. But everyone spoke very guardedly. *And these people all know, but don't trust, one another,* Daniel thought.

After he was waited on, he stopped at a bakery.

Then, heading home with a round, fresh-smelling loaf of German brown bread, he suddenly felt like crying. Although he knew it was foolish, he stopped and asked himself, *How can it be that the* Volk *who make this good brown bread have become so bestial? What could have happened to these people?*

The radio crackled. According to Propaganda Minister Goebbels, pogrom inciter, "The German people's justified outrage at a cowardly Jew's assassination of the German diplomat in Paris expressed itself to a considerable degree last night." Goebbels promised, "This vile act of murder will have further consequences to the Jewish race, to be enacted via legislative means."

Later that evening the Kraushaars' doorbell rang. It was Felix, a young man from the Zionist training camp in Rissen. He said all the men there had been arrested and the camp dissolved. He himself had escaped in the nick of time.

Miriam and Sebastian stayed cooped up with the Kraushaars for the next five days. Except for shopping forays, Daniel, too, stayed in. The Talmud-Torah school was closed till further notice. Most of the teachers had been arrested.

Newspaper accounts of the pogrom went like this: three hundred synagogues burned down or largely demolished; seventy-five hundred stores and warehouses, also numerous apartment houses, incinerated or otherwise destroyed; some twenty-six thousand persons arrested. The number of dead was not given. Taking their cue from Goebbels, the papers called the destruction "a spontaneous expression of righteous indignation from the *Volk*" and burbled that "joy reigns throughout the land because now at least a small part of the Jewish people's crime is avenged." The National Socialist *Kurier* said, "We'll be the envy of our descendants for the privilege of living in these momentous times."

Goebbels's promised "legislative means" soon followed. First, the Reich reserved the right to confiscate all insurance compensation for damage stemming from the Night of Broken Glass. Moreover, a tax of one billion mark was levied on the Jewish Community. This sum was to be offered as atonement for the "cowardly murder" of vom Rath. Furthermore, it was decreed that the Jews assume the cost of rubble removal, including synagogue ruins, and of restoring streets and public places. For Jews to own or manage stores, as well as own or operate motor vehicles, would thenceforth be a criminal offense. Equally punishable would be attending theaters, cinemas, concerts, museums, sports arenas, swimming pools, health spas, and German schools.

WAITING FOR A VISA

THE TALMUD-TORAH SCHOOL STAYED CLOSED for weeks. Rheinhard started feeling stronger and went on his rounds again, trying to sell cattle feed to Holstein farmers. Daniel, Sophie, Sebastian, and Miriam stayed home, but once they'd straightened the apartment, grew restless.

Daniel couldn't concentrate on schoolwork. And there was nothing else to do except to sit together listening to the radio reports of new repressive Nazi actions against Jews.

"Why do the Nazis get so much pleasure torturing us?" Sophie asked one night.

To which Sebastian replied, "Maybe the question should be: Why do people generally get pleasure torturing others?"

Daniel thought back to playing with a friend when he was little. Uli. He lived nearby, in a house with a garden where crawly beasties lived in a little pond. One time they caught a frog, and Uli poked it with a stick. Daniel found a stick too and started poking. The boys kept on till that frog was half dead. Had they enjoyed it? It was interesting, watching a helpless creature react to inflicted suffering.

But when the frog stopped moving, it got boring. Still, they kept on. Because they got mad at the frog. They wanted their fun, and it just sat there, as though dead. That's why they kept jabbing it.

I did that? Disgusting, Daniel thought. "It's a zoological experiment," Uli had said. Bullshit! Torture is what it was.

All right, but what did that explain? They were just children then and hadn't tortured anyone human. Just a frog. Anyway, that night Daniel's conscience had bothered him so much that he couldn't sleep, and he'd made up his mind he'd never do anything like it again.

The Nazis were not children, though, and seemed untroubled by conscience pangs.

But Daniel still assumed, and so did Rheinhard, Sebastian, and Miriam, that the worst was over, that the brutalities would have to stop, or else other nations would surely step in.

Only Sophie took a darker view. "Everything so far was only a rehearsal," she'd said one night.

"As usual, you overdramatize," Rheinhard replied.

However, they now agreed that they should emigrate. Kristallnacht had cured Rheinhard of his reluctance.

But in the meantime, finding refuge anywhere had become nearly impossible.

All the neighboring countries had closed their borders. Some complained that they had already let in too many German Jews. Others, notably Poland, wanted to get rid of its own Jews. Sweden reasoned that it had no anti-Semitism but feared this prejudice might become a problem if it now admitted Jews.

To get into the USA, one needed an affidavit—a sworn pledge of support from a United States citizen. To get in anywhere in Central or South America, one had to bring along great sums of money.

Then, too, one had to have all sorts of certificates and official documents which took months to accumulate, without which one couldn't even apply for the required exit permits. So, by the time one got the last official stamp on the last document, the first document had expired, was no longer valid.

Vienna, Sebastian had heard, was the one exception. There a young official named Eichmann had set up the perfect "emigration machine": He had moved all the different offices and authorities into one large building. And the procedure was simple: A Jew came in through the front entrance, moved from office to office, and exited through the rear door, relieved of every last remaining right, of every single penny, holding a passport in which was stamped: YOU MUST DEPART FROM THE COUNTRY WITHIN FOURTEEN DAYS, OR

YOU WILL BE BROUGHT TO A CONCENTRATION CAMP.

By this method, the Ostmark was able to expel some fifty thousand Jews before the end of 1938, far outdoing the rest of the Reich, which, in that time span, expelled only nineteen thousand.

At the start of 1939, with war imminent, would emigration even be possible? The Kraushaars heard of many people who had managed it, escaping from one day to the next—but how?

Rheinhard got hold of foreign newspapers; he studied want ads, sent out reams of job applications, mailed letters to acquaintances all over the world—with absolutely no success.

Months went by, with no way out in sight. In the meantime, the Talmud-Torah school had reopened. Daniel passed the senior exams, but he was barred from going on to any German university, also from apprenticing in any trade or skill.

All the while Germany kept rearming and made threats against Poland. "If there's war, I'll stick my head in the oven," Sophie said.

Finally an affidavit for the USA. came through, thanks to a colleague of Rheinhard's who had emigrated years before and who had agreed to vouch for them. But the American consulate issued visas according to a rigid schedule, and Rheinhard was told that they would not get their visas until 1942.

Rheinhard argued, pleaded, "Couldn't it be sooner?" but to no avail.

As he was about to leave the building, a consulate employee took him aside and advised him to go to a certain travel bureau on the Jungfernstieg and mention the employee's name.

Rheinhard went there and was told he was in luck. If he and his family took a boat to Havana, Cuba, they could go from there to the United States, even without visas. But they had to act fast and reserve passage right away.

"For when?" asked Rheinhard, and he was told July. This was the only booking still available.

It wasn't quite legal, not a good way to start a new life, Rheinhard brooded. But he had to do it because Sophie made it clear that if he didn't, she and Daniel would go without him.

Only after chasing around for the many required "nonliability certificates" (meaning they didn't owe the state money) could Rheinhard apply for Cuban visas and for emigration permits. The tax on the latter used up all of Sophie's savings. Furthermore, they were required to declare their total assets and make out innumerable official forms listing all their possessions, every last handkerchief and clothes hanger, giving the date of purchase and what it had cost. Then Nazi officials visited the apartment to verify the lists.

Meanwhile, Sebastian and Miriam were still

waiting for permits to immigrate to Palestine. But the British mandate had once again lowered the quota of Jews to be let in.

Discouraged, Miriam and Sebastian decided to try the Havana route. But unlike the Kraushaars, who, thanks to Rheinhard's Aryan status, still had German citizenship, they were classified as "stateless," which made their outlook less promising.

By the time the two were finally granted Cuban visas, all the ships were fully booked until the summer of 1940.

Sebastian worked feverishly trying to get at least Miriam out. He had heard there were ships that smuggled Jews into Palestine. But the Zionist organizations in charge of those ships accepted only people who had finished courses in agricultural training.

In July '39 the Kraushaars were ready. They'd packed their household furnishings into crates, to be shipped to the States once they knew where they'd be living.

They bade good-bye to their remaining friends.

Daniel sought out Peter Mehlhor, the only Christianeum friend with whom he'd stayed in touch, and said good-bye.

Sebastian and Miriam came to the pier to see the Kraushaars off.

On their way to the streetcar that would take them

to the harbor, there was a little incident that Daniel would not forget. They all had much to carry, and a stranger came up to Sophie and asked, "May I carry your suitcase for you?"

He stood in her way, so she couldn't easily pass by.

"We can manage," Rheinhard told him.

"I'd really like to help," the man insisted, loud enough for passersby to hear. "Even if I can't do more than carry a suitcase for you."

Daniel worried that this would cause attention, now, just when they were about to escape.

"Many thanks, but it's not necessary," Rheinhard said. Sophie stepped down off the sidewalk. They walked on.

And the man called to them, quite loudly, "Please know that not all of us Germans condone what's being done to all of you."

They arrived at the pier, said farewell, and embraced—Rheinhard and Sebastian, too. They spoke about a reunion in America the following July. Sebastian and Miriam were determined they would follow.

Later, when Daniel stood at the ship's railing and waved, a senseless hope came over him. Scanning the crowd of people on the pier, he wondered if Armin was standing down there among them. And if not, would Armin still come in time to wave good-bye?

They had not been together since November. They'd run into each other on the street a few times, not stopping, just muttering hello.

Getting ready to leave Germany, Daniel had played with the idea of going to see him one last time. But when he pictured walking through that dark courtyard, smelling the familiar cooking smells, he always decided, *I can't.* And he thought, *No, Armin should come here.*

But then what would I do? Daniel wondered, *Welcome him? Or tell him to go away?*

Armin had not come, and he didn't now. Daniel thought, *He probably doesn't even know we're leaving.*

Sailors removed the passenger bridge, released the thick cables. The horns blasted; the ship drew away from the pier.

As it steamed down the Elbe toward the North Sea, Daniel had a view of the city in which he'd spent his life so far. He saw the steep green Geestrücken; the new, sparkling white town hall; the beach at Övelgönne; the huge crane erected for building the Elbe Bridge the Führer had planned, which was to be bigger than the Golden Gate Bridge in San Francisco.

Sailboats went by and longboats with dockworkers on them and fishing craft that left sharp fish smells in their wake.

Daniel remembered going on excursions to Finkenwerder as a little boy, how excitedly he'd watched the waves and the bubbly froth at the bow of the ship.

Looking across to Altona, seeing all the swastika flags flying not just from official buildings, but from apartment houses and private homes, he tried to hate this land. There were plenty of reasons to hate it. The ship was crowded with people who were fleeing. Many stood on deck. You could tell by looking at their faces how much they had endured in these past years. Quite near Daniel stood a group of men talking about their stays in concentration camps. Every one of these beaten human beings was a reason to hate Germany.

But he couldn't feel it. He felt only a sharp pain, as though something inside him were being cut out, something he already painfully missed and longed for.

IT WAS SEVEN IN THE MORNING, A RADIANT, bright day. The military truck rumbled over the deeply rutted street. I sat in the passenger seat and looked out the window.

For half an hour all I saw left and right was wreckage. Back in Altona remnants of walls were left standing among the bombed-out housing blocks. Here in Hamm, a working-class neighborhood of Hamburg, literally everything had been flattened. How many people lay buried under this rubble?

I turned and watched the driver, an ordinary British soldier. His name was Fred; he was more than forty years old, stocky, with a weathered face and a cigarette between his lips. I called his attention to the rubble fields.

He just nodded and said it was nothing new. He drove this stretch almost daily. I couldn't tell what he was feeling.

When we got to Horner Park, we headed south via Billbrook, through industrial areas that had also been bombed but were being rebuilt. Then we turned onto a wide road lined with fruit trees and drove through Allermöhe, a small cluster of north German farmhouses and a brick church. Cows grazed in the meadows; the wheat stood high. The scene was so idyllic, you'd have thought the war had never been.

As I was leaving Hamburg for the second time, I thought back to the first time, six years before, in the summer of 1939, when we stood on the pier, and Miriam said, *"Auf Wiedersehen,"* as though we'd surely see one another the following year. . . .

Two months later war broke out; no more ships sailed to Havana. So much for Miriam and Sebastian getting to America. They managed to flee to Holland. We got occasional postcards and sent them parcels of clothing and food. But when Germany invaded Holland in 1940, they were trapped again. And in 1942 they were deported eastward "for work detail."

By then we were living in New York. My mother found work as a seamstress. And with help from Jewish organizations, I was able to study journalism.

But I didn't have an easy time starting a new life. This may sound peculiar, but we had lived under threatening, humiliating conditions for so long, it was as though we couldn't grasp how one lived without them. I had to make myself adjust to normalcy again.

My father had fallen sick in Cuba and never recovered his health. When we came to the United States, we didn't have enough money to afford a good doctor, and he grew sicker. What was worse, he'd given up on himself. After leaving Germany, he'd lost the will to fight for his life. He died in autumn 1944. Later, when reports about the death camps reached us, I thought that at least he'd been spared that knowledge.

I didn't know what happened to Sebastian and Miriam. Were they gassed in Auschwitz? Or did they starve to death in a ghetto somewhere? I thought I'd probably never know and tried to resign myself to that. The only thing certain was, they were no longer alive.

But I was alive, riding in an army truck along a small river, leaning my elbow on the open window. Cornflowers bloomed in the wheat fields. And it wasn't quite true that I'd left Hamburg behind, because this flat, marshy landscape with countless canals was also a part of the Hanseatic city.

After a thirty-minute drive we passed through the town of Neuengamme and turned onto a narrow tree-lined road. The huge cinder-block factory where the concentration camp prisoners had labored came into view, then the camp itself, built by the SS in 1938.

Our truck rumbled slowly through an iron gate into a large, dusty courtyard surrounded by barracks. I saw German soldiers standing around in tattered uniforms.

I thought of Sebastian and Miriam again. Were they taken through a similar gate into a similar camp? Did they live in barracks like these? I jumped down off the LKW and was greeted by a British officer. He led me into an administration building. My briefing for my assignment here lasted a scant fifteen minutes.

Five desks stood in a row in front of a bank of windows. The hearings were conducted as though on an assembly line. A German soldier approached my desk, I asked him the prescribed questions: "What Wehrmacht unit were you in? Did you belong to the SS? The Nazi party?" If he said no to questions two and three, he was released, got paid forty mark, and became a free man.

It actually wasn't quite that simple. We'd been instructed to observe the soldiers closely because, of course, they all claimed they'd never been in the SS or in the Party. We were expected to ask certain questions designed to uncover the truth. But having to rush, five minutes per soldier, and overhearing what was said at the other tables made it hard to concentrate. I got distracted—sometimes I completely lost track.

An eighteen-year-old stood facing me. "What was your last rank in the Wehrmacht?" I asked.

"Cadet, noncommissioned," he answered. That meant he'd attended a *Gymnasium*, was in line for a commission, and before joining the Wehrmacht, had held leadership posts in the HJ but was too young to have belonged to the SS or to the Party. I asked about his HJ service. He answered, not moving an eyelash, "I did my duty."

I marveled that under the circumstances he still spoke of his duty with pride, and I was trying to think how I could get more out of him when I heard a voice that I recognized —from the soldier being questioned at the next desk. He was fairly tall and strongly built. He wore an officer's uniform and had a bandage around his head, with straggly blond hair sticking up.

I didn't immediately identify the face. He hadn't shaved in weeks and was deeply tanned. But I'd have known his voice among a thousand others.

I left my cadet standing and went to the next desk. I stood before the German officer and said, "Look at me." He turned my way. Less by his features, which

322

somehow stayed strange, more by the way he gestured, I now recognized him for sure. He looked at me, astonished. Then a smile flickered across his face.

I had to smile too. This person, this face inevitably brought out something warm in me, an instant longing to forget all that had come between us. I had to struggle to suppress the surge of joy I felt.

I scanned the form that my fellow interpreter had filled out:

Name: Armin Hillmann

Wehrmacht Unit #108, Battalion #14, Panzer Division, Sixth Company

SS membership: No

I looked up.

"But you absolutely wanted to join the SS," I said. "They wouldn't take you?"

"No," Armin answered.

I felt he was lying to me.

I grabbed hold of his jacket, unbuttoned it, pulled out his right arm. He let it happen as though he were a puppet.

"Roll up your sleeve," I said.

The whole room had grown silent and was watching.

I took hold of his upper arm, looked for the SS tattoo, and saw a newly formed scab over a wound.

"You left the SS? When? It can't have been longer ago than a few weeks."

"Come on. You know me," Armin said. "You know that I didn't do anything, that—"

True, I knew him well. I was not the right interrogator to conduct this hearing.

"I know nothing about you," I said. "To me, you are any SS man who scraped off his tattoo with a sharp knife."

"I was in a simple battle unit," Armin said.

"That's what they all say," I replied.

I stood there not knowing how to proceed. Armin slipped his arm into his shirtsleeve and shrugged on his jacket.

Twelve years ago I'd stood in a courtyard with this person, painting swastikas on a wall. Was this what I'd come back to Germany for? To see what had become of him?

I looked over at my desk. The cadet still stood there. I looked at the other desks at which the hearings had resumed. I saw the line of German soldiers extending the length of the room, out through the door, and out into the yard, where the sun shone mercilessly down on our tin roof.

Something that my colleague Herman once said

came to mind: "I'm just doing my job here; everything else is no concern of mine."

I'd never quite understood this before. But suddenly I did, and it made sense to me. Armin, supposedly, had also just done his job. And now I did mine. I took the form about Soldier Armin Hillmann, crossed out the *No* in the *SS membership* line, and wrote *Yes*.

I did the same in the next line about Nazi party membership.

Then I went back to my desk, sat down, looked at the cadet, and asked, "Where did we leave off?"

AFTERWORD

THIS BOOK IS BASED ON FACTUAL RESEARCH, but it is a novel, a work of fiction. The people and their experiences are invented, even though they are based on real stories to some degree. I rearranged certain scenes that actually took place, but not the historical events.

Without the encouragement of Thomas Kampe of the London Pascal Theater Company, this novel would not have come to be.

Klaus Humann and Gabriele Leja of Carlsen Verlag gave me extraordinary support during the writing of this work.

Naturally, a great many other people also helped me—people who gave me valuable pointers during conversations or who let me read what they had written about their lives and histories. If I were to name a few, it would mean leaving others out.

The same would be true of published sources. But I want, at least, to mention Victor Klemperer's *Diaries of the Nazi Years, 1933–1945*; Manfred Franke's *Murder Trials*; Ralph Giordano's novel *The Bertinis*; Robert Muller's biographical novel *The World in That Summer*; Karen Gershon's report "The Underchild"; and Erika Mann's "Ten Million Children," about youth education in the Third Reich.

—Daniel Chotjewitz
Hamburg, December 1999